I0644625

AINSLEY
KEATON

The Beachfront Crush

vinci
BOOKS

By Ainsley Keaton

Sconset Beach

The Beachfront Inn

The Beachfront Surprises

The Beachfront Reunion

The Beachfront Secrets

The Beachfront Girls

The Beachfront Sunsets

The Malibu Girls

The Beachfront Christmas

The Beachfront Retreat

The Beachfront Crush

The Beachfront Winery

Vinci Books

vinci-books.com

Published by Vinci Books Ltd in 2025

1

A CIP catalogue record for this book is available from the British Library.
Paperback ISBN: 9781036703790

Chapter One

Ava

Ava was sitting with Sarah, Quinn and Mia on her deck, listening to the waves coming in and out and watching the sun set behind the hills. Julia and Emerson were playing with Bella and Kona, throwing a plastic bone in the water again and again. The dogs eagerly retrieved them from the water and dropped the toys at the girls' feet.

Hallie wasn't with them, because she was having dinner with Conrad. Hallie and her roommate Conrad ending up becoming much more than roommates after all. Hallie was happier than Ava had ever seen her, perfectly content to bask in love with Conrad while thriving at the wellness retreat. She was born to be a counselor, she'd told Ava, and seemed to be born to be Conrad's love interest. Ava was secretly envious of her friend. She found Conrad to be fascinating and complex, a talented artist with a melodious British accent. And Conrad was really crazy about Hallie.

That was plain for everyone to see whenever they were around.

Ava and her ladies were enjoying a glass of wine, the smell of salt and brine in the air. It was an incredibly relaxing experience, just sitting in the silence with her sister, best friend and her best friend's significant other, Mia. Mia was fitting in with the fabric of the friends incredibly well, as everybody knew she would. Mia spent much of her time helping the girls craft songs, with Emerson creating the melodies and Julia creating the lyrics. That project was coming along extremely well, and Emerson and Julia were ready to begin their own YouTube channel. Mia was helping them with that, as well, as Mia had her own YouTube channel. Mia sang and played guitar on her channel, but that wasn't her focus. Her focus was on songwriting and had written songs for many big acts over the years.

Ava was also a bit nervous, because she had to confess something to everybody. She was nursing a serious attraction to Elijah, who was technically her step-brother. Elijah's mother was married to Ava's father, but Elijah had a different birth father. As for Ava, she never even knew that James Bloch, the man who Elijah called "father" was her birth father until recently.

Complicating matters was that Elijah, who was a trauma doctor at Cedars-Sinai, was going East and had invited Ava to come along. He was going to take a sabbatical for the next few months from his job because he wanted to visit his mother in Bridgehampton. She owned a beach house out there, and, because it was January and the off-season, it probably would be quiet around that town. Esther, Elijah's mother, was recently diagnosed with cancer and didn't know how much longer she had left. So, she'd summoned her children to the beach house, because that was where Deborah and Rachel, Elijah's sisters, felt a great sense of comfort.

Deborah was a photographer in New York, and, at the moment, was freelancing. So, she could take the time off to spend with Esther. Rachel was a chef in Bridgehampton, so was already local and had a home of her own in the town, but agreed to stay in the beach house for the month that Elijah and Deborah would also be there. It was understood that this homecoming wouldn't be exactly a happy event. More like bittersweet.

Ava was apparently invited because Elijah wanted her to get to know Deborah and Rachel, Ava's half-sisters. Ava had no relation to Esther, but Elijah still was eager for Ava to get to know her. "My mother is the coolest person around," Elijah said. "And she's 93, so she's seen a lot. You can ask her about Truman Capote." Esther ran with and knew Truman Capote's "Swans," elegant and wealthy women who ran with Truman Capote back in the day. Elijah assured Ava that his mother had many colorful stories to tell about her life.

So, Ava looked forward to staying at the beach house in Bridgehampton. But, at the same time, she was incredibly nervous about the prospect. She'd gotten to know her step-brother and was starting to experience the stomach-churning butterflies she'd only experienced once before - with Daniel, the love of her life, who was tragically killed in a car accident when Ava was pregnant.

And, for some reason, she dreaded telling her friends and family about her feelings. Yet, she felt she needed to talk about it. She knew they thought it would've been strange for Ava and Elijah to date. She'd broached the topic before and they told her as much. But maybe if she told them she was falling for Elijah - and that was how Ava was feeling about him, like she was falling for him - maybe they wouldn't give her such a hard time.

The girls came up to the deck, laughing hysterically about something or another. "Mom," Emerson said to Quinn. "We're going in."

Ava missed everybody living with her. The others - Quinn, Sarah, Julia and Emerson - had recently moved out of Ava's home into their own, newly-renovated Venice Beach home. Since then, Ava had been lonely, even though she entertained superstar actress Fiona Kennedy for awhile while Fiona was hiding out from the paparazzi after a failed marriage. Ava loved having a full and vibrant house, with laughter, music and the occasional meltdown taking place on a daily basis. She was surprised at how much she enjoyed having two 13-year-old girls under her roof. But she did enjoy that, very much. It made her sad to live in her big, empty house all alone.

"Ava, this wine is the bomb," Mia said. It was a bottle of wine created at the Sava Winery, which was Ava and Sarah's winery located in the Santa Monica mountains. It was their Cabernet Sauvignon, a rich red wine that was full-bodied and much milder than many other Cabernet Sauvignons Ava had tried in her life.

"Thanks," Ava said. Then she looked at her glass and towards the now-darkened beach. She took another sip of her wine and closed her eyes.

"Hey," Quinn said. "What's up with you tonight, Ava? I've never seen you so quiet."

Ava shrugged, not quite ready to come clean about her feelings for Elijah. "I don't know. I was just thinking about my trip to the Hamptons with Elijah. I don't really know what to expect."

Sarah and Ava had discussed the prospect that Ava

could leave for a month and they both agreed it was a good time to do so. The grape harvesting was long over, the wines were made and bottled and the crowds the winery experienced during the summer and fall months had slowed considerably. There weren't any events planned at the winery for several more months and, while the winery still did brisk business, it was manageable. So, Sarah was perfectly fine with Ava taking this time off, with the understanding that Sarah would be free to do the same if she ever needed to.

Sarah was looking at Ava with one eyebrow raised. "Uh huh," she said. "I've seen that look in your eyes before. Many times."

"What look?" Ava said in a thin voice. She was transparent. No way could she put one over on one of her closest friends and her sister. Best not to even try.

"You know what look," Sarah said. "And, listen, I've been thinking about it. Yeah, it's kinda weird to be crushing on your stepbrother. But it's not like Greg and Marcia. You were never a part of that family until recently, so you guys were strangers when you met. It's not like you guys grew up together."

Mia just started laughing. "Dude, don't even worry about it," she said. "Seriously. People worry too much about what everybody else thinks. You do you. That's pretty much the advice I've given anybody in my life. You do you."

Quinn looked over at Mia and smiled. Those two were so in sync, Ava thought. They had the kind of easy relationship Ava admired. They laughed at the same things, finished each other's sentences already and just had a comfortable vibe with one another. Ava wondered how they came such a long way in such a short time - they'd only reconnected with one another several months prior- but

Quinn explained they were best friends back in the day and were always like that. They'd always felt a special comfort with each other, like they went way back. Willow, Ava's future daughter-in-law and soon-to-be-mother to her second grandchild, would say Mia and Quinn were old souls linked together in past lives. Willow always said that when two people meet and feel they've known each other for a long time and immediately start talking like friends, it means they were together before.

Not that Ava believed in that sort of thing. Well, maybe she did. After all, she felt that way with Elijah. Right from the start, they conversed like people who went way back. They had a comfort level with each other that was much like with Quinn and Mia. But past lives and reincarnation? Nope, Ava didn't believe in that. She was secretly afraid that this life was all there was. You get one chance to make your mark and then you're gone. You don't come back as somebody else and you don't go to heaven. She wanted to believe there was something beyond this world, but she couldn't make herself believe that.

"Well, sugar, what do you think?" Quinn asked. "You going to be looking at Elijah for the next month with googly eyes?"

Ava smiled as she realized that she didn't have to confess anything to her closest ones. They already knew.

"Am I that obvious?" Ava said.

To that, Quinn and Sarah just rolled her eyes and smiled. "Sis," Sarah said. "You've always been that obvious. I'm your sister, remember? I know all about you. And my memory is longer than an elephant's." She playfully punched Ava in the shoulder. "The question is, what are you going to do about it?"

"Nothing. Listen, I'm going to the Hamptons for a

month and Elijah will be there the whole time. But he's going to be preoccupied with other things, like his sick and possibly dying mother and dealing with two half sisters he doesn't get along with too well. So, I doubt he'll be too focused on me."

Sarah just gave Ava a look. "Better you than me, going back to New York in the wintertime. That's the reason why I think you really have it bad for this guy. You're leaving Southern California in the middle of winter to go to New York. Personally, I think that's crazy, but I wish you the best.'"

Ava laughed. Sarah was right about that. In the middle of January, the weather in Southern California hovered around 65°. She was going to a place where it actually snowed, and snow was one of the things Ava did not miss about the East Coast. Yet she was looking forward to this visit. She had another family. Two half-sisters. Esther was not blood to her, but she'd met the older woman and was completely taken with her. Esther was down-to-earth, funny, lively, and as vital as a 93-year-old woman could be. Now, apparently, she didn't have much time left. While Ava had met her only once, she bonded with her, so she would be very sad once Esther passed away. Not that Ava thought Esther would actually die from her cancer. If there was anybody who could beat cancer at age 93, it was Esther. Besides, it was breast cancer and had not yet spread. It was definitely treatable – just look at Hallie, who beat the very same thing and was in complete remission now.

At the same time, Ava somewhat dreaded the prospect of spending a month with Esther, Deborah, and Rachel. There was a chance that because Elijah didn't get along too well with his half-sisters that there might be some family drama going on. Ava dearly hoped that wouldn't be the case, as there was nothing worse than being in the middle of a family soap opera.

Quinn just smiled and Mia smiled back at Quinn. Ava had a feeling the two of them had discussed her situation with Elijah on more than one occasion. That was the problem with her best friend having a relationship with a woman - two women are going to gossip. When a man and woman are together, the gossiping about one's friends and family usually go nowhere, because the man in a relationship usually couldn't care less.

Ava just took another sip of her wine and turned her attention to the rolling surf. It was now pitch dark outside and the moon was high in the sky. She could hear a distant bark and could smell a bonfire raging just down the beach. She would soon be hearing a different surf on a different ocean as she sat on the deck of a different home altogether. Would she have fun there? Would she be enlightened by her other part of the family? Or would she be caught in some hopeless morass from which she could not get away fast enough?

Ava finally stretched and yawned. It had been a long day at the winery, as most days were anymore. And she was unusually tired. She hadn't been sleeping well at night and often woke up about four in the morning or even earlier, unable to get back to sleep. She didn't know if she just had a lot on her mind or something physical caused her not to sleep well. She would have to figure it out because she was often tired during the day, needing to take a nap while working. That simply wouldn't do – Ava needed her energy.

"I'm heading up," Ava said. "Of course, like usual, you ladies are more than welcome to stay out here as long as you want."

At that, Ava went up to her room and lay on her bed.

But she looked at the other side of the bed longingly. She suddenly realized just how big her bed was. It was a California King and the mattress was a Sleep Number. What was this feeling, that she wanted somebody next to her? It had been so long since she actually had someone next to her in a bed at night. And she really didn't think much about it all these years. Yet, she felt a kind of loneliness that she hadn't felt before. It was as if she was not ready to commit to anybody before and now she was. Something had shifted, and she didn't know exactly why. She only knew it did.

And she knew exactly who she wanted in that bed with her. Elijah.

Oh, she was in trouble.

Chapter Two

Ava

A week later, Ava found herself on a plane heading east. Elijah was already on Long Island, and it was already decided he would pick up Ava at the Long Island MacArthur Airport. Ava being Ava, she tried to protest and say she could just find an Uber over to Esther's beach house. But, Elijah wouldn't hear of it.

"Are you kidding me?" Elijah said, his voice light. "My mom would kill me if I had you get an Uber here. She'd think she didn't raise me right."

So, Ava was looking forward to the drive over to his mom's beach house from the airport. The airport was about an hour away from Esther's beach house, so Ava and Elijah would have a bit of time before riding into the storm. Elijah told Ava that he would be alone when he picked her up. His two sons, Caleb and Levi, wouldn't be at the house at all. They were in school, so Elijah hired a nanny to watch them for the month.

Ava put some earbuds in and settled in for the long flight. She was in first class, so she had a lot of legroom and a place to sleep. Which was important, as this was a red-eye flight taking off at midnight. She would be arriving before 6 o'clock in the morning in Long Island.

She thought about her friend Hallie. Hallie was having the time of her life working at the retreat. And why wouldn't she be? It was really a dream job, helping people better their lives through healthy living. Hallie seemed interested in her roommate, Conrad, an interesting British man and artist who had his own issues with imposter syndrome and fear of failure. Hallie and Conrad had recently started a romance, and Ava was anxious to see where that went.

It seemed that Hallie was attracted to complicated men. Much like Ava herself.

Not that Elijah was complicated, per se. He wasn't. He was a doctor and an amateur photographer who had won many awards for his photography and had been displayed in different exhibits, including winning first prize for one of his photographs in the San Diego Fair. It didn't seem he had any kind of major issues. He just seemed like a normal man.

No, the complication came from the whole incestuousness of it all. Oh, they didn't have any blood relationship. But would it seem weird if they started dating? Would it be odd considering they both shared the same relationship with Deborah and Rachel? Just like Deborah and Rachel were Ava's half-sisters, they also were Elijah's. Elijah, Deborah, and Rachel had the same mother, but not the same father. Ava, Deborah, and Rachel had the same father, but not the same mother. In the Venn diagram in Ava's head, there was some overlapping in the family tree, and that disturbed Ava.

At some point, Ava just decided to close her eyes and

not worry about it. She was overthinking it. As she usually did.

Around 6 o'clock in the morning, the plane touched down at the Long Island MacArthur airport. Ava got off the plane, got her luggage and saw Elijah standing on the side-walk, his hands in his pockets. This dark curly hair had grown out a little since the last time Ava saw him, which was several weeks ago. He was wearing a leather coat, jeans, and a pair of Top-Siders that probably cost over a thousand dollars. He was looking for her, and, when he saw her, a large grin spread over his face.

He looked a little bit like a boy to Ava. He had a youthful face, much like Paul Rudd, a Kansas City boy who made really good. Ava's heart quickened. Boy, this would be difficult staying under the same roof as Elijah for an entire month.

She walked over to him and he gave her a big hug. "Good to see you," he said. "How was the flight?"

"Oh, you know, it was a flight. Pretty uneventful. Then again, flights always are uneventful unless they crash."

"True," Elijah said as he took Ava's suitcase she was wheeling behind her. That gesture, just taking her suitcase without her having to ask, impressed Ava. Maybe she wasn't expecting much from a man after having been married to Christopher, the husband who ended up stealing from her, coming back to try to get back with her, then telling her he'd been married to somebody else while married to her. Christopher was never much of a gentleman, on top of everything else. He was too involved with his own self to think about anybody else. But Elijah seemed to be a guy who was raised right. Not that that surprised Ava. Having met Esther, and having known James, the man who raised Elijah, she thought they probably had decent parenting skills.

"You hungry?" Elijah asked Ava. "I'm thinking we should grab some grub before going into the lion's den." Then he smiled. "Just kidding. I just saw the look on your face when I said that."

Ava wondered if he could tell how nervous she was. And she was out of her element. She spent so many years leaning on her best friends and her sister for support, and they were nowhere to be seen right at the moment. As much as she wanted her security blankets, obviously she couldn't have them and didn't know what to expect when she met her half-sisters. She kind of knew what to expect from Esther, having met her once before, but not Deborah and Rachel.

"I'm actually starving," Ava said. "I haven't eaten since yesterday morning."

"Yesterday morning?" Elijah shook his head. "Why yesterday morning?"

"Well, I kinda forgot to eat. It was a busy day at the winery."

It kind of was a busy day, at that. They hosted a family reunion at the winery that was impromptu, because nobody had made a reservation. Basically, 30 people from the same family just appeared, and Sarah and Ava busted their rear, trying to keep everything afloat. After they were slammed like that, Ava rethought the wisdom of just letting Sarah do everything at the winery while she was gone. So, they both decided to hire a temporary wine tender from an agency.

"Well, come on, let's go get some eggs."

Ava and Elijah then headed over to Elijah's Range

Rover, putting Ava's bag in the back. Elijah opened the door for her, another gesture she wasn't used to anymore. Elijah seemed to be a bit of a throwback with his manners, coming from a time when men opened doors, pulled out chairs and took bags without having to be asked.

Elijah looked over at Ava and grinned. "How does it feel, coming from Southern California to a place that's colder than hell's hinges?"

"Yeah, it's kind of weird coming to a place where I can see my breath. But you forget, I was raised in Kansas City, I lived in New York City for many years, and then I lived on Nantucket, so it's not exactly like I'm a Hibiscus flower that will wilt in the snow. But, I have to admit, I've been a bit spoiled by the Southern California weather. But this is home sweet home for me."

"Well, thank you for coming out. I'm really excited you're going to spend some time with the other part of your family."

Ava knew Elijah probably would've liked to have the same opportunity. But his birth father wanted nothing to do with him, so he never got to know one-half of his heritage. Ava realized she was privileged to have this opportunity and would make the most of it.

"Yeah, here I come, the shiksa in the family," Ava said. She wondered how she would feel about that. While she really enjoyed services like Shabbat On The Beach, because it was such a joyful experience, complete with singing, dancing and camaraderie, all on a beach with the sun setting behind the hills, she still wasn't religious. And she didn't plan on becoming religious. She was still her mother's daughter in many ways. Ava's mother, Colleen, who Ava didn't get along with until just recently, was as practical as it comes. And Colleen was not spiritual or religious, to say the least. So, that was another reason for being apprehensive. She didn't think Esther would judge her for her lack of spiritual beliefs, but would Deborah and Rachel?

"Relax, they don't expect you to know Hebrew or even take part in Friday night Shabbat. My sisters know the score and so does my mom. You don't have to go to temple with us, either. All you're expected to do for this month is to relax and do your thing. It'll be great if you really bond with my family, who's part your family too, but if it doesn't happen, it doesn't happen. Not everybody vibes with each other. So just try not to stress."

Oh, if only it was easy as all that. Ava tended to worry a little bit too much about things that she shouldn't be worried about. Of course, one never knows what is worth worrying about until the thing comes to pass. Sometimes her worries came true.

They got to a bustling restaurant. It was a diner, the kind Ava always liked. She really liked the divey places, the kind of place where truck drivers would come in, park their rigs and eat things like biscuits and gravy, corned beef hash and lots of bacon. She loved that Elijah was taking her to a low-key place like this instead of some fancy place on the beach. It somewhat showed they might have the same taste in breakfast outings.

Ava ordered a traditional breakfast of eggs, bacon, hash browns and an English muffin, with a large orange juice. Elijah ordered some pancakes with a side of eggs. Ava looked around and realized how hungry she was when she saw everybody else in the diner digging into their food.

"Okay, tell me what I can expect when I get to your mother's beach house."

"Well, what can I say? My sisters are there. So, there might be fireworks. Just warning you. Rachel is none too pleased that you got the Nantucket house. She always loved that place and couldn't believe James would give it to what she terms a rando. You watch *Downton Abbey*?"

Oh, that was a question for the ages. Did she watch *Downton Abbey*? Yeah, she watched that show. She'd seen every single episode four times now. She still binge-watched it when she was feeling low. "Of course."

"Well, let's just say Rachel is Mary in the situation and you're Matthew. Without the sexual tension, of course. But, yeah, Rachel thinks you took her inheritance. So, she'll be making backhanded comments about that. Strap on a helmet and prepare to take incoming."

In *Downton Abbey*, at the beginning of the show, Lady Mary's possible inheritance of Downton was given to Matthew, who was essentially a rando because he was a distant cousin of the Crawley family. Mary hated Matthew at first for that reason. Of course, they inevitably fell madly in love and got married, but then Matthew died tragically in a car accident. Mary's getting back on her feet after such a tragedy made up much of the storylines over the subsequent seasons.

"Oh, great. Just what I wanted to hear, your sister already has it out for me."

"Just fair warning. Deborah won't hassle you about the house, though. So, who knows, you and Deborah might be allies against Rachel."

Then Ava smiled. "Well, just remember, Matthew and Mary eventually fell in love and got married, even though Matthew took Mary's inheritance, as it were. So, you never know, maybe Rachel and I will become the best of friends. But thanks for the heads up. I'll be prepared to kiss Rachel's rear end."

"Well, it's not as bad as all that. You're not going to

necessarily have to kiss Rachel's butt. In fact, I think you shouldn't. You should probably just ignore her kvetching. And that's all it is – kvetching. That's just how she is. She's a chef, you know. I could just imagine what she's like working. Probably a female Gordon Ramsay without the charm."

Ava laughed. "That's a great picture in my head. Gordon Ramsay in drag and with no sense of humor."

Elijah smiled with a twinkle in his big brown eyes. "Sounds like a pretty accurate portrayal of Rachel."

The food came around and Ava and Elijah dug in. The eggs were amazing - light, fluffy, prepared with butter and seasoned just right. The bacon was crisp and the hash browns were also crisp on the outside, tender on the inside. The orange juice was freshly squeezed. Elijah cut off a part of his pancakes, which were tropical and infused with banana, pineapple and coconut, and put it on Ava's plate.

"Try this," he said. "It tastes like Hawaii."

Ava smiled and took a bite of his pancake and then rolled her eyes with pleasure. "Oh my God. If Hawaii tastes like this, I want to go to Hawaii. That's all I can say."

Elijah smiled. "You've never been to Hawaii?"

"No, can't say I have. But it's on my bucket list, along with going on a European river cruise that stops in Prague."

"Prague? Why Prague, exactly?"

Ava shrugged. "It just looks like a beautiful city." Unlike Ava's sister, Sarah, Ava was not a world traveler. She always wanted to be, but before she landed on Nantucket, she was way too busy raising her triplets and working all the time. So, she'd never been to Europe, even though she always wanted to. And Prague always looked like the most beautiful city in Europe to her.

Elijah winked. "Well, we should go to Prague sometime.

I could show you around. My family originated from Czechoslovakia, so it holds a special place in my heart."

Ava took a deep breath and turned her attention to her food. As much as she wanted to tell Elijah that she would love to go to Europe with him, she couldn't bring herself to say the words. At any rate, Ava was sure Elijah was just making the offer about going to Prague lightly and in jest.

"That would be a lot of fun. And I could probably do it now. The winery I own with Sarah is doing really well and we just found a wind tender who is temporarily working for our winery. I hope she turns out to be somebody we could permanently hire."

"Oh, the flexibility of somebody who owns their own business. I envy you. Me, I have to take a sabbatical whenever I need an extended vacation." Elijah continued to dig into his pancakes, adding extra syrup. "I'm on vacation," he said with a smile. "Time to live a little and add more syrup."

"Oh, it's always time to add more syrup," Ava said, taking a sip of her freshly-squeezed orange juice. "Life's too short not to."

Ava agreed with that sentiment. Life really was too short to not add more syrup. She raised her glass and Elijah clinked his with hers. "To a new family and new beginnings."

Elijah smiled. "I like that. I hope you can get close to this part of your family tree. Everybody deserves to be loved and accepted by their blood. And, by the way, my mother absolutely adores you. She told me the two of you got along famously."

Ava smiled. "We did. I think your mother is an amazing woman."

"Yeah. She's 94 this Saturday and still walks three miles

every day. She gets around her brownstone in Brooklyn better than people half her age. She's always told me that age is just a number, and it is. That's no cliché - it's true. Even though my dad is gone, and she mourns him every day, she's in no hurry to join him in the afterlife. She has too much living to do right now." He sighed. "She has breast cancer, but it's Stage 1. She's being dramatic when she says she doesn't have much time left. I think she's just saying that to get her family to spend some time with her. Mission accomplished."

Ava thought about the YouTube video she once saw of a woman who was over 100 years old and dancing a line dance at somebody's wedding. She was the sweetest older lady Ava had ever seen and Ava thought how wonderful it would be if that were her at age 100 plus. Dancing at the wedding of her great granddaughter, whoever that might be. It sounded like Esther, Elijah's mother, might be that 100 plus old woman boogying with 20-somethings on the dance floor.

"Well, it sounds like you have some excellent genes," Ava said.

"Yep. I'm the son of a Holocaust survivor and a 1950s-era socialite. They both have such fascinating stories to tell. And they both were extremely healthy into their 90s. My dad was, you know - healthy. He had no health problems we knew about until he had his fatal stroke. But that's how you should try to live life. Be healthy until your last day and then go quickly. We should all be so lucky."

Ava sipped her orange juice and dug into her eggs with gusto. "I guess as a trauma doc you see people all the time who aren't as lucky as your mom and dad, huh?"

Elijah shook his head. "Oh, you don't know the half of

it. It's draining seeing so many people with gunshot wounds and car accident injuries. That's all I really see, too. I've lost a lot of patients on the operating table and that wears on me, too. Especially the children." He shook his head again and his face got visibly agitated. "Like the 9-year-old boy I treated who was shot by his 5-year-old sister. His sister thought the gun was a toy. It wasn't locked up or even hidden and the parents were too strung out on drugs to care."

"That must be so difficult," Ava said, putting her hand on his. "Did that boy make it?"

"No," Elijah said. "The sister's in foster care, of course, but she had her own trauma. How does something like that wear on your psyche as you get older? Killing your brother like that? One boy is dead and one girl's life is ruined. All because of stupid, careless parents who had no business having kids in the first damn place."

Elijah's face clouded over, his usual sunny demeanor replaced by a furrowed brow, a frown and a shaking head. He took a deep breath, drank some more of his orange juice and appeared to compose himself somewhat.

"Anyhow," he said with a smile. "I'm not going to think of that 9-year-old boy or his 5-year-old sister on this vacation. It's time to turn my brain off and just enjoy myself."

"I know," Ava said. "I know how hard it is to turn your brain off. I'm pretty Type A myself. For most of my life, I've worked my tail off, so much so that it was difficult to relax. I didn't know what to do with myself when my 'Sconset Inn was slow and I was sitting on my hands a lot of the time."

Ava's heart raced slightly as she looked at her stepbrother's handsome face. She loved his thick curly hair, his big brown eyes with the strong eyebrows and his bow-shaped lips that were now curled in a contemplative frown. Dammit, why did he have to be so attractive?

"Well," he finally said. "It sounds like we both will have problems unwinding. To tell you the truth, I wonder if I can last long with Rachel under the same roof as me. I never got along with her." He looked sad. "And God I miss Val. Val was my partner in crime. We were close in age, just one year apart, and she used to sneak out of the house with me at 2 AM to go and smoke cigarettes and swim in the ocean. She would find out when high tide was and we'd go surfing at that time, no matter what time of the morning it was. So, if the tide was high at 2 in the morning, that's what time we would sneak out of the house."

"I'm so sorry about Val," Ava said. She hired Val's daughter Jessica to work at the 'Sconset Inn. Jessica was currently planning a wedding to Andrew Jameson, the international pop superstar who loved her as a child and loved her now as well. Jessica had the trauma of seeing her mother killed by an errant bullet meant for Andrew himself. That trauma, buried for many years, led Jessica to drug addiction. She had since overcome her addiction with the help of AA, and was mentally healthy and would be working on a degree in Marine Biology at UCLA. She'd come a long way.

"Yeah, me too," Elijah said. "But Jessica is doing fantastic. You played a large part in her recovery." He nodded and smiled. "If you turned her away when she showed up at your door, she probably wouldn't have made it. Jessica's father and stepmother are both jerks. I mean, who turns their back on children who are hurting and need you? Yes, she was battling drug addiction, but her father should've understood and tried to get her help instead of shunning her."

Ava smiled. Elijah burned with anger at injustice. Just like it was unjust that a 9-year-old boy was killed by his 5-year-old sister because of their parents' negligence, it was unjust that Jessica was left to battle her addictions alone. Well, she wasn't alone, but only because Ava got involved.

"I had to take her in," Ava said. "I knew she was on the edge the first time I met her. And I took her house right out from under her nose. What kind of a person would I be if I told her to pound sand?"

"Well, it was a kind thing to do regardless," Elijah said. "Don't minimize it."

The waitress came around and brought the check. Elijah quickly picked it up and waved Ava off. "I got this," he said.

"I insist," Ava said. "After all, you're giving me a free vacation. In Bridgehampton, no less."

"Oh, yeah, that's such a prize," Elijah said. "It's January in Bridgehampton. There's snow on the ground and it's 20° outside. You could be in Southern California in 60° weather and no snow. Believe me, this won't be the greatest vacation for you."

Elijah paid the check over Ava's protests and raised his eyebrows. "Come on, let's go into the lion's den." Then he smiled. "Just kidding. Only Rachel's gonna give you a hard time."

They got into Elijah's rental car, a brand-new Range Rover. The seats were leather and plush and this car was tricked out with everything. It was a kind of car that started at $200,000, Ava knew. It was probably the kind of car her old clients drove. Before she came to Nantucket to run a bed-and-breakfast, she was a high-powered attorney who helped billionaires cheat on their taxes. She imagined those greedy guys driving a car just like this. Not that Elijah was like them or had anything in common with them. So far, he certainly did not seem to have anything in common with her greedy clients.

Ava hoped that was correct.

Chapter Three

Ava

Elijah and Ava arrived at Esther's beach house a little bit after noon. Ava was very nervous, mainly because Elijah told her just how angry Rachel was with her for taking that house. But she was looking forward to seeing Esther again. Elijah was correct that Esther, at age of 93, was full of life. Indeed, as if to prove Elijah's point, Esther was on the beach doing yoga when they arrived.

"Hey, Elijah," Deborah said when she saw Elijah and Ava come up the porch of the house. "Mom's on the beach," She turned to Ava. "She has a yoga instructor come three days a week to put her and her friends through their paces. She's 93 going on 30, what can I say. By the way, I'm Deborah, and you must be Ava."

Deborah extended her hand and Ava shook it. Deborah was like a female version of Elijah in some ways. Like Elijah, she had dark curly hair and big brown eyes. Her face was freckled, giving her a youthful look, and she was lithe and thin. She looked like she did daily yoga herself. She was wearing a flowing caftan with a colorful scarf.

Elijah rolled his eyes and smiled. “Mom does yoga year-round. That’s probably why she’s still so fit and trim. But only Mom loves to do yoga on a snowy beach when is 30° outside. I’m surprised she gets a group together to do the same.”

“Mom says the cold invigorates her. And she loves this house so much because it’s right on the beach and likes to take advantage of that,” Deborah said.

Ava furrowed her brows. She remembered, distinctly, that Esther told her that she didn’t care from the beach. Ava had a conversation with Esther because she needed Esther to sign off on Ava’s plan to sell the Nantucket house early. According to the terms of the will under which Ava got that house, Ava was not allowed to sell the house for five years. Ava wanted to sell early, so she had to get Esther in on the plan. Esther told her that she was not upset about Ava getting the Nantucket beach house because she didn’t really care for the beach.

“That’s strange,” Ava said. “When I met Esther she said she didn’t care for the beach.”

“Mom not care for the beach?” Deborah said. “On what planet?”

Ava knew the most likely reason why Esther told her she didn’t care for the beach was because she didn’t want Ava feeling bad about taking the Nantucket beach house. Which told Ava all she needed to know about Esther. Esther was evidently a woman who was altruistic and fair. Of course, Ava knew that instinctively. It just confirmed it for her.

“I don’t know.”

Elijah took Ava’s suitcase and walked up the stairs. Ava looked around, and was impressed by the charm of the house. It was an older house, probably built around 1920, and had the features of a house built during that time. The wraparound porch, the crown molding, the hardwood floors, the small kitchen, the formal dining room – these were all 1920s era home features.

Deborah took Ava's hand and led her to the sunroom that opened up to the beach. "This is my favorite part of the house," she said as she went over to the French doors and opened them wide. The sound of the ocean filled Ava's ears. In the distance, Ava could see a group of ladies on the beach with a young and fit thirtysomething man leading them through Vinyasas. They went through their sun salutations - forward fold, plank pose, chaturanga, upward dog, down dog, another forward fold, then mountain pose.

Ava watched them on the beach for a few minutes, admiring that Esther was 93 and battling cancer and still doing sun salutations with the energy and vitality of a woman half her age. "You know, my sister Sarah is big into yoga. And she's gotten my best friend Hallie into it too. I've never done it myself, but I probably should. I would love to be in my 90s and taking a yoga class from a hot young guy."

Deborah smiled. "That's Kevin. He owns a yoga studio in town and comes to people's houses and does private instruction on the side. You should meet him. He has the kind of calm reassurance that you want from a yoga instructor. He has that whole mind-body connection thing down pat."

Elijah joined them in the sunroom. "Where's Rachel?" he asked.

"She went to town to get some stuff for supper this evening," Deborah said. "Rachel is a chef here in town at a five-star restaurant. She'll be hanging around this house for the next month or so, because she's taking vacation time.

But she still loves to cook, even for just her family, so be prepared for some wonderful gourmet meals. If you're a foodie, you'll love staying with us this month."

"That's true," Elijah said. "I don't always get along so well with Rachel, but she has her good qualities. And one of her good qualities is her cooking ability. And the fact that she loves to do it. A lot of times, you'll find a professional chef who wants to eat peanut butter and jelly in their personal life because they're are so damn tired of cooking all day. That's not Rachel. She's always on."

Ava looked forward to staying with the Blochs, anyhow, but she really got excited when she thought about an entire month of gourmet dinners prepared by somebody else. Not that Ava would just sit on her rear and let Rachel do all the work. It wasn't in her nature to be a bump on a log and just let people wait on her. She would certainly chip in wherever she could. But she imagined delicious dinners and good company around the dinner table, and looked forward to that.

"Nothing wrong with that," Ava said. "If I was a professional chef, I would probably be the same. Because nobody wants to eat bland food or the same food all the time. And I love to please people and make them happy. And one of the best ways to make people happy is through their stomachs."

"Be prepared to be quite happy," Deborah said. "If good food does that for you."

Just then, the yoga class was apparently over. Esther, dressed in long pants and a light pullover, her gray hair cut very short above her in ears, her yoga mat in her hand, walked up the walkway leading from the beach to the house. She saw Ava and waved.

When she came up to the house, she gave Ava a huge hug. "I'm so glad you could join us," she said. "When Elijah told me you were coming to visit us along with him, I got very excited. I wanted to get to know you better ever since I found out about your existence. It was my biggest regret that James never let me get to know you. But, now you're here, and you're part of the family."

Deborah raised an eyebrow. "Yeah, with me and Rachel, you're literally part of the family. I can't say it's not strange to have a half-sister that you didn't know all these years. But it is what it is. I'm sure we're not the only family to go through this. Anyhow, I agree with my mom. It is good having you here. Everybody should get to know their family. Better late than never."

Just then, Ava heard a new voice. "Hey," a woman said. "What's going on?"

Ava turned around. There, standing in front of her, was a woman in her early 50s. Presumably Rachel. Like everybody else in the family, she was tall and thin. However, unlike Deborah and Elijah, Rachel was blonde and her hair was straight. Her eyes were blue. She almost didn't look like she was a part of the family. Other than her tall and lithe frame, she looked completely different from Elijah and Deborah.

Rachel raised an eyebrow at Ava. "Hello. I presume you're Ava."

Ava felt very nervous about meeting Rachel, mainly because Elijah was so adamant about Rachel not being happy with her for getting the Nantucket beach house that Rachel loved so much. She almost wished Elijah never said anything about Rachel's feelings about the matter. Then again, if Rachel was unhappy with her, and Rachel would make Ava's stay very uncomfortable because of it, Ava should probably know that going in.

"Yes, I am. And I assume you're Rachel."

She nodded. "Yes, you're very astute. Then again, it's a process of elimination, isn't it? You met Deborah and you know my brother. Now here I am, so I must be Rachel."

Rachel had a big grocery sack in her arms and Deborah followed her into the kitchen so both of them could unload the food. Esther put her arm around Ava and walked with her into the living room. "I was warm on the beach, even though it's really colder than a witch's tit. But, you know, you start moving your body out there and you can't feel the cold. But now, I'm feeling chilly. I think I need to make a fire."

Nothing sounded better to Ava at that moment than the opportunities to sit in front of a roaring fire. It was chilly outside, in the low 30s, and the hearth room looked warm and inviting. Ava and Esther, walking arm in arm, went into the hearth room. Esther bent down and lit a fire and put a large log on it. The hearth room featured of large stone fireplace in the middle, high ceilings with wood beams, and beautiful leather furniture surrounding the fireplace. Oriental rugs were scattered around the room, and a golden retriever was relaxing in front of the fire.

"Meet Max," Esther said, petting the dog. "I just got him. He's a rescue and is the sweetest thing you'll ever meet." She continued to pet him, and the dog wagged his tail eagerly as he rolled on his back so Esther could scratch his tummy. "Do you like dogs?"

"I love them. I don't have a dog right now, but I plan on getting one when I get back to California."

"You should. People don't always appreciate how much a dog brings to your life. It's not just unconditional love, but there's something about a creature that needs you that's very appealing. Let's face it, you raise children and the children are going to do what they're going to do no matter how much you try to guide them. They are who they are. But dogs, all they want is to be loved by you and will turn out perfectly if you do one simple thing - love them. Simplicity at its finest."

Ava knew the pitfalls of trying to guide children into a spot they didn't want to be in. As much as she wanted her children to go in certain directions - she wanted Charlotte to get a Masters degree in art to make her bachelor's degree in art count; Samantha to get a college degree in some kind of field that would pay well and provide stability; and Jackson to also get a degree in a lucrative field with stability – they all went their own way.

Charlotte had a baby and got married when she graduated from college, and now was a stay-at-home mother and part-time ghostwriter with a semi-unstable husband who already bolted once and, for Ava's money, was likely to do it again, leaving her daughter high and dry.

Samantha, on the other hand, landed on her feet. She was a highly sought-after wedding cake decorator, but, for years, Samantha was spinning her wheels and Ava worried about her constantly.

Jackson chose the most unstable field of all - acting. Ava hated Jackson's field of choice, because Ava knew the reality of trying to make it in Hollywood. Actors, even the successful ones, always seemed to be one box office bomb or failed series pilot away from obscurity. And that was if they were lucky enough to actually land a series or a movie. Most of them never stopped waiting tables. So even though Jackson was starring in a highly anticipated biopic about Zelda Fitzgerald, and was getting great notices from people who had seen the dailies of the film, Ava knew the reality. Jackson would never have a stable life in the field he chose, but acting had always been the only thing he'd wanted to do. So, Ava could not dissuade him, nor did she try. She knew it would've been futile if she did.

Ava joined Esther on the floor and scratched Max's ears. The dog sighed happily and stretched. He almost had a smile on his face.

"Yes, you're right. A dog will never give you trouble, and they're so trainable. Unlike children. But your children seem to all be doing quite well. I think you did a wonderful job in raising them."

Esther nodded. "I suppose so. At least, if you think about their professional lives. But their personal lives haven't been nearly as successful. They're all divorced, because they all chose the wrong person for them. Elijah married a gold digger and made the mistake of having kids with her. Deborah married a man who's distant, critical and nothing she did ever made him happy. Rachel married a man who refuses to grow up, which meant he had no interest in being there for a wife and kids. He was too busy chasing after every skirt he could, buying new cars he couldn't afford because he refused to find a steady job, and expected Rachel do all the child care and housework even though Rachel busted her tail at the restaurant 6 days a week while he lounged around the pool drinking margaritas with his bimbos."

Ava was familiar with the concept of marrying the wrong person. She did that with Christopher, her second husband who robbed her blind. He tried to come back, but Ava wasn't having it, especially when he explained that he married somebody else, and had kids with this other woman, while married to her. Still, they were friends. Christopher had called her a few times to ask her advice on a new woman he was seeing. Ava was tempted to tell him not to pursue anybody at all, because he wasn't relationship material and he shouldn't subject anybody to his neuroses, but she listened and gave advice to him. She didn't hate the man at all. She just was done.

Ava shook her head. "Smart women, foolish choices, huh?" She remembered reading that book back in the day. Daniel, her first husband, had just passed away in a car accident and Ava was dating. But she was meeting a lot of losers, so she read that book. It was very enlightening, and after reading a book she realized there were a lot of people who needed to never be in any relationship at all. Christopher was one of those people, but was going to do what he was going to do. Ava just felt sorry for anybody who might get involved with him in the future.

Esther shook her head. "Don't I know it. Not that James and I had such an easy time of it. Obviously. If we did, you wouldn't have been around. But the important thing is that he was willing to work at our marriage. He messed up, I messed up, we both hurt and betrayed one another in profound ways. And if he wasn't willing to put in the work with a counselor - and we saw a counselor regularly for over 50 years - we wouldn't have made it. Not in a million years. And that was the difference between my relationship with James and my children's relationships with their spouses – the two of us were willing to work on the relationship. All my children managed to marry people who had no interest in that. All of my children's spouses resisted all requests to work on their marriage, so they all got divorced."

Esther stoked the fire a little bit and the flames licked a little higher. The dog rolled over on his stomach and licked Ava's hand. Ava smiled and petted his soft fur. "So, your kids are all on point with their professional life, not so much with their personal. I guess that makes sense. After all, it's so much easier to control your professional life than your personal one. Just because it's so much easier to control how well you do in your profession but you cannot control another person."

Just then, Elijah showed up. "Hey," he said. "You two look like you're having a cozy day in front of the fire. That's the perfect way to spend today because the forecast calls for more snow. So buckle up. I know you're not used to it these days because you live in Southern California, and maybe you never wanted to see snow again after leaving the East Coast. But here it is. And by the way, Rachel just made a delicious lobster broth. That's her specialty, things made with lobster. You'd think she grew up in Maine, not Brooklyn."

"Lobster broth?" Ava asked. "That sounds amazing."

"Yeah," Elijah said. "I know, Jews eating lobster, what is the world coming to? But we aren't strict in this house when it comes to kashrut laws."

Rachel was now in the hearth room as well. "It is amazing. It's made out of lobster shells, white wine, fish stock, tomatoes, onions, carrots, and celery. A little bit of tarragon, a bay leaf or two. It makes for a wonderful light lunch when combined with freshly-baked sourdough bread. Elijah told me you guys ate a big breakfast, so maybe a light lunch is just what you want."

All at once, even though Ava didn't realize she was hungry, her stomach rumbled. She wasn't hungry, but the prospect of eating a lobster soup sounded.just too wonderful to pass up.

Elijah smiled. "I told you. While you're staying here, you're going to be eating very well. I hope you don't get spoiled."

Ava smiled. "I can assure you, I will be spoiled. I live alone now. Nobody to cook for me." She missed Julia, who loved to bake. Ever since she left, Ava was not only lonely but was faced with the reality that not only was nobody going to cook or bake for her, but, because she lived alone and had no one to cook for, she wasn't motivated to make gourmet meals at the house.

The upshot was, if nobody was coming over to have a glass of wine on her deck, Ava lived on take-out food. She was always looking into meal prep plans like Blue Apron and probably would subscribe to such a plan in the end. But, right now, it was just too depressing to just be on her own and not have people to cook for. She somehow felt that subscribing to a meal prep service would mean she was admitting she would be alone for the rest of her life. Of course, it didn't mean that. She was just feeling sorry for herself.

Esther and Ava put out the fire, and followed Elijah, Rachel, and Deborah to the screened-in dining room. There was a formal dining room, with a large table and 10 chairs around it. And then there was this dining room, an informal one. It was attached to the sunroom and its floor-to-ceiling windows looked out onto the beach. Despite the chill in the air outside, it was nice to have the French Doors flung open with the sounds of the ocean roaring in their ears.

Rachel brought out a turine and a loaf of bread. She spooned, with a large ladle, some broth into everybody's waiting bowls. And then she sliced up the bread, buttered each slice and handed everybody some of the warm crusty bread. "Hope you like it," she said to Ava.

Ava dipped her spoon into the broth and closed her eyes. This broth was delicious and hearty. Ava loved lobster and she always did. But she never thought of the possibility of using the lobster shells for anything, let alone make them into a soup. But the lobster, combined with the wine, the herbs, and the vegetables, was delicious and aromatic and paired beautifully with the warm bread.

Ava rolled her eyes in ecstasy as she took spoonful after spoonful of the beautiful broth. "This is amazing," she said. "Where did you get the idea to make a broth out of lobster shells?"

Rachel smiled. "I studied in France. At the Le Cordon Bleu in Paris. French cooking is my specialty. So, if you like lots of wine and butter, and foods made with these staples of life, you'll have a very good time here for the next month."

What Rachel was saying was heaven to Ava's ears. French cooking with lots of wine and butter? Yes, please! She was very impressed that Rachel studied the Le Cordon Bleu in Paris. Ava knew something about that particular culinary school and knew it was one of the best in the entire world. That school was where Audrey Hepburn's character Sabrina went to, and Ava could imagine Rachel in the role of Sabrina, with a demanding French chef putting her through her paces. Julia Child herself went to the place.

"Do you speak French?" Ava asked.

Rachel rolled her eyes and shook her head. "No. I just went to France like a typical American and expected everybody to speak English. Yes, of course, I speak French."

Deborah looked at Ava sympathetically. "Don't mind her. She's just kind of an absolute snob about people who can't speak more than one language. Like myself. I mean, I speak Hebrew, of course, but no other language. In Rachel's eyes, I'm an absolute Philistine."

It was then that Ava looked over at Rachel and realized she was glaring at her. It was probably true what Elijah said to her about Rachel. Rachel clearly hated her.

"Well, I guess I'm really a Philistine, because I only speak English myself," Ava said sheepishly.

"You were a lawyer, working for a large firm, and you never learned another language?" Rachel asked pointedly.

"Leave her alone," Elijah said to Rachel. "Not everybody speaks another language."

Ava wondered if Elijah himself spoke another language. She would have to ask him some time. She imagined he probably did. After all, he used to work for Doctors Without Borders. At the very least, he probably had to communicate with the locals, so he probably knew Swahili or some other similar language.

"No. I never really had to learn a different language when I was working my job. I never traveled overseas for my job and if I had a client from a different country who didn't speak very good English, I usually got a translator for him or her," Ava said evenly.

Deborah got up and came back in with a bottle of wine and five glasses. "I don't like to day drink, and it is the early afternoon, but I think this conversation will call for it. Besides, we're all on vacation, so a little day drinking won't hurt any of us."

Deborah poured a glass of wine for everybody and Ava took a sip.

Rachel raised her eyebrow at Ava. "So you're a typical American, are you? Can't be bothered to learn about other cultures or other languages because everybody should just get with the program and learn our language and our culture?"

Ava opened her mouth, but Elijah stood up. "Rachel, that's enough," he said. "Ava never said she didn't want to learn about other cultures. She just said she doesn't know another language."

"You know lots of languages," Rachel said to Elijah. "You know Italian, French, Spanish, Yiddish and Hebrew. That's because you care about the world. Then again, you're not the kind of guy that would steal somebody's house, so you're automatically a better person than my half-sister."

Esther was quiet during this interaction, surprisingly enough. Ava wondered why.

But the older lady finally spoke up. "Rachel, we all know what this is about. It has nothing to do with whether or not your half-sister Ava is a Philistine who doesn't care about the world. And I, for one, want to address this situation head on. There's no need to be passive aggressive about any of this. And, for my money, passive aggressiveness is toxic. I'll have none of that under my roof. We will have a peaceful vacation living together but the only way that will happen is if we speak to one another openly about what's bothering us."

Ava took a deep breath. She loved that Esther was so direct. And Esther was absolutely correct. Rachel *was* being passive aggressive. Her cutting comments to Ava were the very definition of passive aggressiveness.

Esther turned to Ava. "Okay, let's just get this out of the way. I'm sure you know Rachel resents you for accepting the house on Nantucket. We've had a lot of talks about this. I've explained to her, time and again, the reason why you got that house. Now, I would like to ask you for your feelings about getting the house."

Rachel stood up and pointed at Ava. "You've told me all about it, Mom, but here's the thing. As I understand it, Ava, when you accepted the house as part of the will you had no idea my father was your father. Isn't that right?"

Ava felt she was being cross-examined on the stand. It

was just the way Rachel was badgering her and it didn't help that she used the phrase "isn't that right?" That phrase was a classic cross-examination phrase that Ava used time and again with recalcitrant witnesses on the stand.

Ava cleared her throat. What could she say? It was true that she accepted the will without question, never even considering that there were possibly other heirs around who would resent her for doing so. And it was true that at the time she accepted the house in the will, she had no idea James was her father. She just thought he was a kindly old man who wanted to reward her for her work for him over the years.

"Yes, that's true," Ava said.

"And there is a way to decline a bequest in a will, isn't there?"

Obviously, there was a way to decline a bequest. You have to file a signed and notarized disclaimer with the probate court. So Ava did have a way of declining the bequest if she decided to. And, maybe morally, she should have. Maybe morally she should've at least done more research on the house – who would've gotten the house if she didn't and why James would've done that.

"Yes. That's true, I could have declined it if I wanted to."

Rachel sat back in her chair. "I knew that. I saw an attorney after you got the house, of course. My father and I had talked about this house and I was under the impression I would get the house once he passed away."

Esther rolled her eyes. "I have no idea why Rachel believes that," she said. "And she hasn't explained it to me."

Rachel took a sip of her wine. "I did tell you about it. Dad and I had many talks about that house. At that time,

Jessica was living there. I told Dad I would take care of her. You know he was very worried about her."

Esther looked embarrassed. "Oh, poor Jessica. Nobody told me what was going on with her. If I would've known what she was going through, I would've taken her in myself. I don't know why everybody thought that hiding that from me was the right thing to do." She shook her head. "I only found out recently that she was battling drug addiction when she lived in that house by herself."

"Mom," Deborah said. "Nobody knew what was going on with her. Nobody but Dad. So, don't blame yourself."

Esther shook her head. "I do blame myself. I was so judgmental about Jessica. I didn't know she was struggling with addiction and PTSD about her mother's death. I just thought she was lazy and not self-directed and I really didn't want to enable that. I feel so guilty about the way I treated her."

"Well," Rachel said. "Nobody knew she was addicted to OxyContin. The only thing we knew was she wasn't working and had dropped out of school, and Dad thought it was his duty to make sure that Valerie's daughter was not living on the streets. Everybody thought Jessica should just pay the price for her bad decisions, not knowing what was causing her bad decisions, but I told Dad I would take care of her. I was the only one in this family who believed Jessica should be taken care of by somebody else even though she was an adult. And that was why Dad was willing to give me the house."

Elijah put his arm around Ava protectively. "I'm like everybody else in this family because I was oblivious to Jessica's struggles. But I have an excuse. I was working overseas at the time all this was going on. But I want everybody to know that Jessica is on her feet, thanks to Ava. Ava took her in and gave her structure and a job. Now she's flourishing and engaged to be married. Ava didn't need to do any of that. She certainly could've turned Jessica away when she appeared at Ava's door, but she didn't. She didn't because she has a big heart. Now, Rachel, I think you need to lay off her. Our niece is not dead in a ditch somewhere because of Ava."

Esther looked at Ava approvingly. "That really was a lovely thing you did for my granddaughter. I think it's time for that particular rift to also come to an end, so I think I'm going to get in touch with Jessica this evening and invite her to come out and stay for a while as well. I just wish everybody would've told me about her problems. And I should've paid more attention myself to her struggles. But I thank you, Ava, for helping her when she had such a great need."

Rachel was glaring at Ava. It looked like she was ready to blow a gasket. This entire conversation was boomeranging on her and it was apparent she didn't like it one bit. Somehow, someway, everybody sticking up for Ava was making things worse.

Ava knew she had to stand up for herself. "Rachel, I apologize for accepting the bequest of the house. I'm not going to try to justify it, because, if I do, it's going to sound incredibly selfish. The truth of the matter is, I was desperate and wanted to start fresh someplace new. When I got the bequest of the house, I thought my prayers were answered. I just lost my job and knew I probably couldn't find another job that would pay enough for me to survive."

Deborah spoke up. "Ava, you really don't have to justify it to us. You did just what anybody else in your situation would've done, including Rachel. There's hardly anybody would get a house willed to them and just turn it down. So, there's no need to justify and no need to feel guilty. And when the truth came out about why you got the house, I understood it. James was your father. He was just as much your father as he was ours. Just as much. So you had just as much right to that house as any of us did. There's no need to apologize for it and Rachel needs to back off."

Elijah nodded. "I agree with Deborah. Ava had just as much right to the house as you did, Rachel. In fact, she had more right to the house, because, after all, our father gave her the house. He didn't give it to any of us, just her."

"That's because she's Dad's bastard child," Rachel said. Her words were starting to slur, which told Ava that Rachel was starting to get a little drunk. "And I'm just saying what everybody around this table is thinking, so don't even get on me about this."

And there it was. That was the root of Rachel's hostility. She wasn't angry at Ava. She didn't know Ava and it wasn't rational to be angry with Ava because Ava did what anybody else would've done and did not deny the bequest. No. She was actually angry with her father for having an affair with Ava's mother and then covering up Ava's existence all these years. She couldn't tell her father how she felt, so she would take her rage out on Ava, the innocent party.

Ava understood on a deep level exactly why Rachel was saying these cruel and horrible things. However, nobody else understood. That was evident by all the hell that broke loose after Rachel called Ava "Dad's bastard child."

"Rachel," Elijah said. "I don't know what your problem is, but I suspect you've been drinking and not just here at the table. I suspect you've been drinking all day. Because, if you're sober, what you just said has zero excuse. If you're drunk, you need to sleep it off and apologize to Ava when you wake up. If you don't do so, I will never speak with you again."

"I second that," Deborah said. "If you want to have a relationship with either of your siblings, I suggest you do as Elijah says and sleep off your drunk and apologize to Ava today."

Esther did not join in the pile-on, however. Ava thought there was a reason for that. "Ava, why don't you and I go to the sunroom? I think this lunch is done and everybody can clean up the mess. And I'm not just talking about the food."

Esther and Ava went to the sunroom together, leaving behind the three siblings yelling at each other. Rachel was telling Deborah and Elijah that she wouldn't apologize because it was true, and Elijah and Deborah were laying into her about being unnecessarily cruel to the half-sibling she just met.

"I needed to talk with you about Rachel," Esther said as she shut the French Doors.

Chapter Four

Esther

Esther knew she would have to say something to her youngest daughter Rachel. She hoped it wouldn't come to this, which was why she didn't talk to Ava earlier. But, with the blowup around the lunch table, it was clear Esther would have to step in and become the mediator between her daughter and Ava, who technically was not her daughter, but Esther somehow felt she was.

Esther sat on one of the wicker chairs in the sunroom, which was her favorite room of the house because it faced the beach. She opened the solid glass door so she could hear the ocean waves rolling in through the screen door. Even though it was quite chilly outside, only 30°, Esther didn't feel the cold. Since it was clear Ava did, however, which was to be expected because Ava was used to 60° weather during the wintertime, Esther offer her a blanket. Ava gratefully took the cashmere blanket Esther offered and wrapped it around her shoulders while she sat on the chair.

"I wanted to apologize for Rachel," Esther said. "And I don't want you to think she hates you. She doesn't. She doesn't know you."

Ava nodded. "I think I understand."

"Maybe you do." Esther took a deep breath. "Of all the children, Rachel had the most trouble with what happened between her father and me when I had an affair and so did James. Rachel was not even born at the time I had the affair and so did James, but the aftermath of that caused deep and lasting wounds that didn't heal for at least ten years."

Esther was always very open with her children, and now she thought maybe that was a mistake. She and James went through intense marital counseling for many years after their respective affairs and children born out of wedlock. And it was difficult for Deborah, Rachel and Valerie to understand what was going on. It was also extremely difficult for Elijah because he was the product of Esther's affair, which was one of the reasons for the marital strife.

The tension in the house was such that it could be cut with a knife for many years, including during Rachel's formative years. So, when everybody was old enough to understand, Esther and James set all of them down and explained their affairs. Deborah was angry about the affairs for a long time, too, but she understood when she had her own extramarital affair. Deborah and Esther recently made peace with what had happened between James and Esther all those years ago, because Deborah finally understood the reasons for having an extramarital affair in the first place. Deborah realized she was being judgmental of her mother and father and that having extramarital affairs don't always mean the ones having the affairs are bad people. Sometimes affairs are a cry for help and a symptom of a much larger problem.

But Rachel never understood and never forgave. And Esther recently found out why Rachel was so rigid about her beliefs about what happened between Esther and James. Basically, Rachel was depressed because she never got over Valerie's death and she somehow blamed Valerie's death on her parents.

Her rationale was convoluted but apparently made sense in her head. Rachel said she invited Valerie to the Hamptons house on the weekend Jessica turned 5 years old. Everybody was gathering there that weekend for a family reunion. Rachel was excited about the gathering, even though she was still angry with her parents, because she wanted to see her extended family.

Valerie, however, wasn't formally invited to the shindig because Valerie refused to speak with her parents during that time. They had horrible arguments about Valerie's relationship with her husband, a rich jerk who knocked Valerie around. James informed Valerie that Valerie's husband was not welcome in any space he was in, so Valerie curtly informed her father that if her husband couldn't be around, neither would she. Esther thought James was being harsh and they had a huge fight about this - Esther thought that turning their backs on Valerie would backfire and make their daughter hate them. James wanted to demonstrate tough love. James won the argument and Valerie wasn't invited to the reunion.

Rachel really wanted Valerie at the reunion, so she personally begged her sister to come that weekend. But Valerie would not relent. She said she would not visit her father until her father accepted her husband. Esther, for her part, agreed with James that Valerie's abusive husband was unacceptable, but didn't agree with James' tactics. She wanted to use visits to their Brooklyn house and their

Hamptons house as a way to subtly bribe Valerie to at least seek help in her marriage, even if Valerie wasn't willing to divorce her husband. Yet, she also was desperate to see her daughter so was willing to back down on her demands that Valerie seek marriage counseling.

For James, Valerie's husband crossed the red line when he hit Valerie on several different occasions. James told Esther that he knew marriage counseling wasn't appropriate in this situation. Once an abuser, always an abuser, and James didn't want that man anywhere near him ever again. In short, the whole thing was a mess and resulted in an estrangement between Valerie, Esther and James.

The rest was history. Valerie didn't come to the Hamptons that weekend for the family reunion but chose to stay on Nantucket. Because she was on Nantucket, she was in the park where she was murdered. In other words, if James and Esther, especially James, were not so rigid about accepting Valerie's husband, Valerie would be alive today.

As for Jessica...everybody in the family was desperate to get her away from her father. Everybody was terrified that Jessica would be the brunt of her father's abuse now that Valerie was gone. Esther and James saw lawyers to inquire about getting custody of Jessica, and they even filed a custody suit, but they had no standing and no proof of the abuse. So Jessica's father moved with Jessica and his new wife down to Florida, effectively cutting Jessica off from the rest of the family. Heartbreak piled on heartbreak.

Rachel blamed Jessica's estrangement from the family on James and Esther, too. After all, if Valerie weren't murdered in the park, Jessica and her family would still be living close by on Nantucket and they wouldn't have been cut off from young Jessica's life. The dominoes had fallen, and the brutal results from James' decision not to invite

Valerie for the family reunion were endlessly cascading. Rachel never got over any of it.

Esther told Ava that whole sad story.

"So, Rachel has never forgiven her father," Esther said to Ava. "Rachel and Valerie were close as two sisters could be. They were only a year apart and Deborah is four years older than Rachel. So Rachel and Valerie naturally bonded because they were so close in age and just had personalities that meshed well together. In other words, Rachel and Valerie were best friends as well as being sisters, and nothing could ever replace that. When Valerie was killed, Rachel told James it was his fault. Valerie would still be with us today if she would've come to the Hamptons instead of staying on Nantucket."

"I see," Ava said. "So, I think I understand the root of her anger. It's not rational, but I have a feeling Rachel felt entitled to the Nantucket house as a peace offering and a way for her father to apologize for Valerie's death. And, when I got the house, she felt cheated. The house was a proxy in a way. If he would've given her the house, it would've represented to Rachel that her father cared enough about her feelings about Valerie's death to do something to make peace with her."

Esther nodded. "Yes, I think that's true. I don't pretend to know the complicated psychology of my youngest daughter. I don't think even she understands exactly why James giving you that house was such a betrayal in her eyes. But I can tell you that she sees it as a betrayal, and, as I said, because James is not around for her to yell at, she's going to yell at you. I just don't want you to take it personally."

"Believe it or not, I don't," Ava said. "I've been through enough counseling through my life because of my own estranged relationship with my mother to know that people are not always rational and don't always see things realistically. I understand James' reasons for banning his daughter from his homes. It's the tough love thing. He was essentially blackmailing her, but for the right reasons."

"Yes, that's true," Esther said. "James was beside himself that Valerie stayed with that man. He was very sensitive to violence against others because of what happened in Germany to our people, including to his best friend Morty Savich. He heard the horror stories from Morty about the concentration camp and knew what hatred and violence can do to a human psyche. He didn't want that to happen to his daughter, so he was desperate to use every tool in the toolbox to get her to leave her husband. Of course, nobody knew what would happen that weekend. You can't dream that something like that would happen to Valerie when she chose to stay on Nantucket instead of coming to the family reunion here in the Hamptons. And James felt extremely guilty about Valerie's death. He did not need Rachel to pile on, but that's what she always did."

Ava took a deep breath. "Thank you for telling me this."

"Well, I figured I had to. I don't want you to feel you're not welcome here. I consider you to be part of my family. As crazy as that sounds, I feel you're almost my daughter. And, of course, you are half-related to both Deborah and Rachel. With Deborah, I think you'll be just fine. She understood James's motivation for banning Valerie and her husband from the house that weekend. She agreed with it. She hated Valerie's husband as much as everybody else did and all of us were afraid Valerie would end up dead by her husband's hand, ironically enough. Deborah never blamed James for what happened to Valerie. Deborah only blamed the gunman. And she also blamed lax gun regulations, and has become an activist about banning assault rifles. In other words, Deborah looks at the whole situation rationally. Rachel doesn't."

"So, what do you suggest? I'll be under the same roof as Rachel this month. And, you're right, she is my half-sister. So how do you think I should approach this so we have a relationship?"

Esther sat in the chair, seeming to consider that question. And then her face lit up. "Well, I mentioned it before, but I think it'll be a lovely idea. I'll invite Jessica and her fiancé to come and stay for a few days. Have you been in touch with her? Do you know if she could visit?"

"She probably could. She's living in Los Angeles, and next semester she's going to complete her master's degree at UCLA in marine biology. At the time when she was hurt in that skiing accident, she was scheduled to start her master's program in marine biology at Boston University. Then she was in a skiing accident, became addicted to OxyContin, and dropped out of life. She was accepted to the UCLA Marine biology program but doesn't start until the fall. So, right now, she's running a YouTube channel about her passion, Marine biology, while she waits for school to start. As for Andrew, her fiancé, he's in between touring and recording and taking a little break. They could both come out here to the Hamptons right now. It would be the perfect time for them, actually."

Esther clapped her hands with delight. "That would be perfect. It's time to reconnect with my granddaughter. I hope she doesn't hate me for turning my back on her when she needed me. I'm ashamed to admit that I was practicing the same tough love with Jessica that James practiced with Jessica's mother, Valerie. I let her sink on her own. We all did. We all failed her. But, if she came out to visit, I have a feeling she could be the bridge between you and Rachel.

And, in the process, I could get to know my granddaughter again."

"I'm close with Jessica still," Ava said. "Would you like me to call her and invite her out?"

"Would you? That would be such a dear thing to do."

So, Ava called Jessica, who eagerly accepted the invitation. "James and I were wondering what to do with ourselves right now," Jessica said over the phone. "James is not due back in the recording studio for another month, and, as you know, I don't start school until the fall. We were talking about taking a trip, and coming to the Hamptons sounds like a wonderful idea. I've been thinking about my family lately, so it seems like serendipity for this to happen right now. I have to talk to James, but I'm sure he'll be on board with it too. I can't wait to see you and everybody."

"Jessica said she would love to come out," Ava said after she hung up the phone. "She was really excited when I asked her."

Esther smiled. "Sounds like it's time for everybody to come together again. Time to heal some family rifts and time for everybody to make amends." Then she hesitated. "I'm not saying I'm at the end of my life. But I'm 93 and have breast cancer. It's stage one, but at my age you never know. That's why I had everybody here this month. And it would be perfect if I could say my goodbyes to Jessica, if it is time to say goodbye. I'm surprised I didn't think about that before."

Esther and Ava came out of the sunroom and nobody was around. Lunch was apparently over and everybody had scattered to different parts of the sprawling house. So, the announcement that Jessica would soon be a part of their motley crew would not be made until later that evening.

Ava was excited that Jessica would join them. And she

knew Esther was even more excited. Esther knew she needed to become close with Jessica, because she was right - Esther and her children all abandoned Jessica when she needed them most. Jessica was a good person with a warm heart and generous spirit. She didn't deserve to have everybody shun her.

Ava hoped the reunion between Jessica and her family would bring closure and healing to everybody. If anybody deserved closure and healing in their life, it was Jessica.

Chapter Five

Jessica

Jessica got off the phone with Ava and was beyond excited. She would finally be reunited with her family. Not with her father, because he was still not taking her phone calls. But with her grandmother, her aunts, and her uncle.

Jessica understood why her grandmother, aunts, and uncle didn't support her when she needed them. She knew her grandfather James understood she was battling drug addiction. But Jessica asked him not to tell her grandmother Esther, her aunts Rachel and Deborah, and her Uncle Elijah. She was ashamed. So, they didn't know she was struggling so much in her life. It was therefore really her fault that she drifted away from the family. If she would've been open and honest with them about her struggles, she knew her grandmother Esther at the very least would've been in her corner.

She was no longer ashamed of her life. She had been clean for well over a year. She was in a very healthy relationship with Andrew Jameson, her childhood friend and current international pop star who was known the world over. Andrew was booked for a stadium tour in the summer as the headliner and would be traveling all over the world for the better part of year. Jessica was not looking forward to being separated from him for so long, but Andrew assured her they would make it work. He loved her completely and thoroughly, and she felt the same way about him. Of course they were madly in love. After all, they were very close as children and both had a major crush on one another when they were four years old. Fiona Kennedy, the Hollywood actress turned bookstore owner and matchmaker, confirmed that Jessica and Andrew were made for one another.

So Jessica knew on every level of her being that Andrew would not be unfaithful to her on tour and would never been unfaithful to her. She knew this. So her apprehension about him going on tour had nothing to do with her not trusting him. But it had everything to do with her possibly feeling lonely without him. They had been inseparable ever since they found one another Nantucket. They started out as very good friends. Jessica was still reeling from her drug addiction and was in AA. As such, she was not supposed to get involved in a romantic relationship for one year. That was the mantra around her AA group. The first year after quitting drugs or alcohol or any kind of addiction was reserved for recovery. Anybody who might end up derailing that recovery was not welcome. Not that Andrew would ever derail her recovery, but Jessica still didn't feel ready to jump into a relationship with him for a full year after she quit OxyContin.

But their friendship, which was a deep friendship because the two were matched on a soul level, blossomed into a passionate romantic relationship after the first year of Jessica's sobriety. She received her one-year chip from AA, and, that very evening, the two made love for the first time. And it was just as wonderful as she thought it would be. Andrew was gentle and caring, his poetic soul coming out with every kiss. It was a beautiful, magical night. The very next evening after that, Andrew asked her to marry him. He told her he always knew he would marry her, from the time they both were kids together. At four years old, when he was hanging out with Jessica every day, he told his mother that he would marry her one day. Not that he really knew the concept of marriage at that age. He only knew he loved his best friend. That's what he told Jessica - that he knew from the age of four that she would be the one in his life until he died.

Just then, Andrew was home. He had gone to Venice Beach to buy a new guitar. Jessica was going to go with him but had to work on some content for her YouTube channel, so she stayed home. He walked into their house and kissed her on her lips, which is what he always did whenever he came home from anyplace he was at. He told Jessica that he never wanted to come home to greet her with anything less than a special kiss.

"Babe," Andrew said. "I wrote a song on the beach today. I walked out of the guitar shop and was just inspired. Would you like to hear it?"

That was a silly question. Of course she wanted to hear it. She always wanted to hear his new songs and give him feedback and input. Andrew often told her she was his inspiration, his muse. He was noticing his songs were centered more and more around the concept of true love. His songs prior to meeting her were more about other things than a romantic love. They were about more esoteric issues because he had never been in love before he reconnected with Jessica. But now his songwriting was focused around how he felt about his fiancée Jessica. So, of course she loved hearing his songs. She loved how she was reflected in those songs. She aspired to live up to her image reflected in those songs and knew that she had become a better person because she didn't want to let him down.

"Love to," Jessica said. "But honey, I have some news. Actually, I was hoping we could talk."

Andrew went into the living room and put his guitar next to the fireplace. "All ears," he said.

"Ava called me. She's staying with my grandmother for the next month in Southampton. Esther has a beach house, and my uncle and aunts are staying with her also. So they want me to go out there and stay with her as well, and you, too. What do you think? We were talking about taking a little trip this month. I know we weren't really thinking about going to a cold place. But, at the same time, I think I would love to see my family. It's been too long."

To Jessica's surprise, Andrew was not jumping up and down with joy about Esther's invitation. He looked worried. "Jessica, don't get me wrong. I think it's a wonderful thing you have a chance to re-connect with your family. But I've always wondered why they were not in your corner when you were recovering. You never talked about that. You talked about your father turning his back on you. But you never talked about your grandmother and why she would do that. I just don't want you to be disappointed."

Jessica took a deep breath. "I'm not sure, to be honest. I know my grandfather didn't tell my grandmother about my drug addiction, because I asked him not to. And I just didn't reach out to them when I was in the throes of addiction. That was on me, 100%. I went to stay with Ava and never called my grandmother to tell her what I was doing or where I was. I was completely ashamed. I didn't reach out to my grandmother and she didn't reach out to me."

"That's what I'm saying," Andrew said. "They had a chance to help you with recovery and they didn't. Now you're completely recovered, your life is together, you're getting married to me and you're starting your masters program in marine biology in the fall. You're healthy and whole. And now Esther wants to reach out and see you. I don't know how I feel about that."

"What do you suggest I do? Keep shunning them when they're reaching out to me? I don't have a time machine, so I can't go back in time and make it to where we healed our rift a long time ago. As I see it, I have one choice and only one choice if I want to be a part of the Bloch family again. I can accept this invitation, which I'm sure was made in good faith, and make the best of it. It hurts that I was left to sink into my addiction alone, but there's nothing that can be done about it now. The only thing that can be done about the rift between myself and my family is to go to that Hampton's house with an open heart and forgiveness and let them love me if they're going to."

Andrew was always very supportive of everything Jessica wanted to do as long as what she wanted to do was not self-destructive. So he smiled and gave her a kiss on her cheek. "Okay, then. Let's go to the Hamptons."

Jessica felt very excited. Her insides were doing happy flips. "Really? You don't mind going out there?"

"Of course not. I just want you to be careful around those people. I know they're your family. I know you love them. But I just don't want your heart to be broken. You've had enough sadness and tragedy to last a lifetime. That's all I'm saying."

So Jessica and Andrew made plans to go out to the Hamptons that very weekend. Andrew made the arrangements, getting on the Travelocity site and booking tickets for them. "It's done. And, believe or not, I've never been to the Hamptons. I don't know how I feel about going there in the dead of winter, though."

Jessica smiled. "It'll be just like going to Nantucket in the winter. You know how Nantucket during the summer is a madhouse, but during the winter, it's quiet and peaceful? I'm sure the Hamptons are the same way. I'm sure the Hamptons summertime is just as nutty as Nantucket in the summer. And I'm also sure the winter is quiet out there, with just the locals and none of the usual tourists and people coming from the city on the Jitney."

Jessica felt a calming sense of closure was about to be realized. She had her life together. She had a great love. She was going to start her master's program in the fall. She always felt the only thing missing was the love of her family.

And now it seemed she would finally have that again.

Chapter Six

Ava

After Ava had her talk with Esther, and everybody was gone from the lunch table, she went to find somebody to talk to. She wanted to talk to Elijah, but if she couldn't find Elijah, she would settle for talking to Deborah.

She found Deborah in the hearth room, sitting in front of the fire. "Elijah and Rachel went into town," Deborah said. "They asked me to go, too, but I felt I should stay behind. I figured you would be looking for everybody so you had to have somebody around to talk to."

Ava smiled. "Thanks for that, that's very considerate."

"Well, I wanted to get to know you. Elijah already knows you, and Rachel, well, I'm sorry about that. At any rate, Elijah knows I want to talk to you. So, that's part of the reason why he left with Rachel." She stoked the fire a little. "By the way, where's Mom?"

"She went to take a little nap. She told me she got up

early this morning and her yoga class took a lot out of her. So, she's a little tired."

Deborah nodded. "Yeah, Mom gets tired easily. It could be because she's 93 years old and it could be her cancer treatment." She looked sad. "You know, no matter how old you get, your parents are your parents. And it will be hard to lose them no matter old they are. When Mom passes on, whether from this disease or 10 years from now when she dies skydiving or surfing or something like that, it'll be heartbreaking for all of us kids. Sometimes I think of that when I see her struggling. And, believe me, she struggles even though she tries to hide it."

Ava thought of her own mother. For so long, she didn't like her mother. She always loved her but didn't always like her that much. They never saw eye to eye, mainly because her mother irrationally blamed her for the way her father treated Colleen. Ava's father was James Bloch, not Kenny Flynn, the man she always thought was her father. And Ava suddenly understood her mother's lifelong hostility towards her. That went a long way in healing their rift. Now they were close. Her mother was even talking about marrying her current girlfriend Barbara and wanted both Ava and Sarah to stand up for her at her wedding. Ava never thought something like that would ever be possible just a few years ago. Hell, a few years ago, Ava never would've imagined her mother marrying another woman, because the fact that her mother was a lesbian was another secret her mother kept from her.

So many secrets… But she knew what Deborah was saying. Her mother was in her early 70s and was very active on the federal bench. It didn't seem her mother would be passing on anytime soon. Yet Ava knew when her mother actually did pass on, Ava would feel like an orphan.

"I know what you're saying," Ava said to Deborah. "You're never ready to lose your parents, are you?"

Deborah shook her head. "No. You're certainly not." Deborah turned to the fire and stared at it for a few moments. "I guess my mother had a talk with you about Rachel?"

"Yes. She did. And I understand Rachel's hostility. I always know hostility doesn't just spring out of nowhere. It's usually irrational, but it's real in that person's mind. And I understand Rachel is really angry with me as a proxy for the anger at her father. I don't know what to do about that, though."

"I don't know, either. I talked to her before you got here and begged her not to attack you. She told me she wouldn't, but obviously she didn't listen to me. Oh, I guess people will do what they're going to do. I think she couldn't help herself. But don't take it personally. Believe it or not, she's a wonderful sister and friend. And I think she will be to you the same. Just give it time."

Ava nodded. "Jessica will join us. Maybe that'll help things along."

Deborah looked pensive. "Jessica. I'm surprised she wants anything to do with us. We weren't exactly there for her when she needed us."

"I know. But there's a chance for everybody to come together for a little while."

"Maybe it will help with Rachel. Rachel and Valerie were very close, as I'm sure my mom told you."

"She did. But I wonder why nobody wanted to help Jessica."

Deborah took a deep breath. "Only Dad knew what was going on with her. And he took that secret to his grave."

Ava didn't know what she was talking about. "I don't understand."

"Dad never told Mom or any of us what was wrong with Jessica. So we didn't know. Mom found his journal after he passed away. And she read it. He talked all about Jessica and her addiction in the journal. My mother felt so guilty after she read that journal. She just came across it a couple of days ago, however. So, prior to finding that journal, she just thought Jessica was lazy and not wanting to work, and she and all of us resented her for mooching off our father. We didn't understand and I guess didn't really want to understand. So her coming here will probably be the best thing for everybody. Including Rachel."

"Rachel said she wanted the house because she wanted to take care of Jessica. It was one of the reasons why she resented me for getting it."

"I'm sure she was just saying that. Rachel felt the same way all of us did about Jessica at that time. All of us have always been expected to make our own way in the world. That was one thing my parents really instilled in me. Instilled in all of us. We were all to uncover our talents and use them to the best of our abilities. None of us were supposed to ever just sponge off other people. Sponging off others is a cardinal sin in this family. So, I became a photographer, Rachel is a chef, Elijah a doctor. Ironically, at least with Rachel, the only person sponging is her ex-husband. Bastard not only cheated on her and made her do all the housework and childcare, but didn't work and is suing her for alimony of all things."

Ava couldn't believe what she was hearing. Rachel's husband cheated on her, didn't work, expecting her to do everything around the house and now was wanting alimony? What the hell?

"Why did Rachel marry a man like that?" Ava asked.

Deborah sighed. "Why indeed? Why does anybody fall in love with anybody? The heart wants what it wants, but I think I've learned the brain needs to be involved much more than the heart in these situations. If the brain is telling you a guy is a loser, but your heart is going pitter patter, you better listen to your brain. Because the heart will steer you wrong more often than not. I learned that myself."

Ava nodded. "And so did I."

Deborah cocked her head. "I don't want to be impertinent. But I was wondering – do you have a thing for Elijah?"

Ava swallowed. Was it that obvious? She hoped it wasn't but apparently it was. If Deborah saw Ava's attraction to her stepbrother, Rachel probably did as well.

"Why do you ask that?" she asked nervously. She felt her heart pounding and her hands shaking. It was obvious by her reaction to the question what the answer was. But she still hoped she could hide it. If nothing else, she wanted to hide it from Elijah himself. She had no idea how he felt about her and probably didn't want to know.

"It's just the way you look at him. Elijah is a very attractive guy. And the two of you have no parents in common, unlike you and I and you and Rachel. If you have a crush on him, that's perfectly fine. None of us will judge you."

Ava sighed. By the way Deborah was talking, it was obvious Elijah didn't feel the same way about Ava as Ava felt about Elijah. If he did, Deborah probably would have said something different than to say that if Ava had a crush on Elijah she wouldn't judge. She might have encouraged it between them if Elijah felt the same.

Then again, maybe Elijah did feel about Ava the same way Ava felt about him but never told his sisters that. Still, if

Deborah could see the attraction on Ava's face, couldn't she also see that about Elijah? Deborah obviously was a perceptive woman. And because she apparently had the female intuition, she probably would've sensed the same vibes from Elijah as she was sensing from Ava. She apparently didn't, so Ava assumed her ardor was unrequited.

"Yes," she confessed. "He does seem to be my dream man. That seems so ridiculous, coming out of the mouth a 55-year-old woman."

Deborah seemed sympathetic. "I know what you're saying. We should have it all figured out by now, life. But we never really do figure it out, do we? Show me a woman who claims she doesn't act like a middle-schooler on occasion and I'll show you a liar. At any rate, I say go for it. I think you and Elijah would be great together."

Ava felt herself blush and took a sip of her water. "I don't know. I think Elijah isn't interested."

Deborah nodded. "Don't worry that you're not Jewish, if that's the issue. Elijah doesn't care about that. He doesn't plan on having more children. His kids are Jewish because their mother is. Judaism is passed down from the mother. If he wanted more children, it might be an issue, but it's clearly not. So…"

Ava wanted to change the subject. "What time will Rachel and Elijah get home?"

Deborah shrugged. "No clue. As I said, Elijah wanted you and I to get to know one another. We're sisters, after all. Half-sisters, anyhow." She smiled. "So, tell me everything about you. Your hopes, your fears, what keeps you awake at night. And I'll tell you the same."

So, for the next several hours, Ava and Deborah delved into each other's psyches and souls. Ava told Deborah things she hadn't expressed to anybody else in a long time, even her best friends. She told her about her fear of failure, her fears that her children would somehow become unhappy, her hopes that her winery would continue on its successful path and that her mother and she would continue to be friends. She carefully avoided the issue of her hopes for romance, though. Not just because her romantic history represented a distinct failure, but also because she wanted to avoid further excavating her feelings for Elijah with Deborah.

Deborah talked about her fears that her relationship with her husband would negatively affect her boys. "I wasn't a very good role model for them. I stayed in a relationship with a man who only found fault all the time. And I'm so afraid they'll just repeat the pattern set by their father. I don't know if I could forgive myself if they became just like their father and treated their wives the way my husband treated me. Other than that, I guess I'm happy. I'm a photographer and I love it. It's not the most stable profession in the world. I have to rely on selling my work to various photo sites. I also have a website, and I sell stuff on Etsy. I get some wedding gigs, too."

And then Deborah giggled. "Do you remember Glamour Shots?"

Ava rolled her eyes and smiled. "Oh my God, talk about a blast from the past." Truth be told, Ava was guilty of getting a glamour shot herself. She distinctly remembered being made up in so much makeup she felt like a streetwalker and dressed in barely-there clothes and négligées. It was fun getting made up, in a way. Even if she didn't look like herself at all in the resulting photo. What wasn't so fun was when the salesman tried to high pressure her into getting multiple pictures she couldn't afford. The whole thing would've cost her hundreds of dollars, back when she was 16 years old and working at the mall on minimum wage, which was $3.35 an hour back then. Needless to say, she couldn't afford that. But she did buy one photo. She still had that photograph hidden away somewhere, a testament to the silly idea that she could ever be anything other than what she was. A plain, simple, but fresh-faced redhead with too many freckles.

"Oh, do I. Why do you ask?" Ava asked.

"No reason. I just thought about that. Because, and don't laugh, but my doing a glamour shot back in the day was what got me interested in photography in the first place. I don't know, I wanted the feeling of making somebody's day. Making somebody feel pretty, if only for an hour or two. I liked what the photographers did. I never really understood why Glamour Shots went out of business. I guess it was just distinctly an 80s phenomenon. Anyhow, I do a version of the glamour shots now. A tasteful version, however. I like to photograph pregnant women, with their special glow. I like photographing nudes. A lot of women like to have a studio photograph done of them completely naked so they can look back on their hot younger self when they inevitably get older. I also really love photographing weddings. I love capturing hope."

Ava realized that Deborah was the rarest of creatures. Love had disappointed her but she still believed in it. That was obvious. Ava asked to see some of her work, and Deborah brought it up on her laptop. And it was obvious that Deborah had a special knack for capturing hopeful emotions. Whether it was love for one another, or love for oneself, Deborah brought it out in her photographs.

"Do you think you'll ever marry again?"Ava asked Deborah.

Deborah chuckled. "I'd like to. I know I was in a terrible

relationship with somebody who found fault with everything I did all the time. But I don't think I'll repeat the same mistake. As I said, I believe in love, but I also believe in intellectually analyzing the next relationship. I just can't avoid red flags and try to ignore them. That's a recipe for disaster. Red flags are what you look for. I won't avoid them next time."

Deborah told Ava that her sons Samuel and Asher were together in Europe, backpacking around. "I think it's lovely and romantic, but the mother in me hopes they take their experiences in Europe and apply them to something worthwhile. Asher is only 18, but of the two of them, he has a better head on his shoulders. He's keeping a travel blog going and he's video documenting everything along the way for a YouTube channel he wants to start when he gets back. As for Samuel, he's kind of a slacker and doesn't have any ambition to speak of. I worry about him."

Ava nodded. "Don't worry. He might find his footing." And then Ava told Deborah about Samantha and how Samantha was always a big worry for her but got it together. "The important thing is, at least to me, let the kids have their space to figure things out. Maybe they'll figure it out or maybe they won't. I think I've learned that whether or not they figure things out, my pushing them wouldn't help a bit. As much as I would have liked to have pushed all of them to become engineers or doctors or lawyers or some type of professional person with a stable income, it just wasn't in them to do that. And I needed to back off."

Elijah and Rachel finally pulled up and came into the house. "We got more stuff for the dinner tonight," Elijah said.

Rachel came over to Ava. "Ava, I have to apologize for how I acted earlier. It's not you. I'm just going through something. Truth be told, I really don't care about the house. I just care about what it represented." She blinked. "I care that my father didn't care about me enough to tell me what he was about to do with that house."

Ava nodded. "I understand."

"Yes," Rachel said. "And I'm really not angry for myself as much as for my mother. My mother really should've gotten the house. Not you, not me. My mother. True, I love the house more than anybody in the family. It reminded me of Valerie. We spent a summer together there, just Val and I, and there are so many memories wrapped up in that house. Memories of Valerie and I staying up late talking, going to the beach, chasing after boys. It was a simple time and I thought it would last forever. So, yeah, losing the house to what I thought was a perfect stranger, you, stung. Because I felt I was losing Valerie somehow. But I know it was selfish of me to believe I was entitled to the house. But my mother really should've gotten it. To tell the truth, I felt giving it to you, the symbol of my father's betrayal, was what really hurt the most."

"What Rachel's trying to say is that you're an innocent party. Rachel misplaced her anger and she realizes it. We had a talk. I hope you can forgive her," Elijah said.

Ava shook her head. "Really, there's nothing to forgive. Rachel talked out of turn, but really, it's no big deal."

Deborah smiled at Rachel. "I'm happy you have a different attitude now. By the way, Jessica is going to visit us, as well."

Rachel nodded but then Ava noticed tears in her eyes. "I'm happy for that. I love Jessica. I just wish we had her mother still around. It's so unfair what happened to Valerie."

Just then, Esther came into the hearth room and joined

everybody. "What did I miss? I'm sorry, Ava, that I wasn't around today. I just get so exhausted after my yoga class. It's not easy for an old lady like me to be put through her paces on the beach when it's cold. I mean, the cold is invigorating, don't get me wrong. It makes me feel alive to do that. But it takes a lot out of me. It's not as easy to recover now as it was when I was younger. Younger and not going through cancer treatment."

Ava put her arm around Esther. "Esther, don't worry about it. I just want you to go at your pace with me being around. I don't want you to stress about having to entertain me or anything else like that. Just go at your pace."

That evening, they had a pleasant dinner. Ava thought she saw Elijah stealing glances at her when he thought she wasn't looking.But was that her imagination? Her imagination sometimes got away from her, even at the age of 56 years old.

She wondered if that would ever change.

Chapter Seven

Jessica

"Jessica, I have an idea," Andrew said as he and Jessica packed for their long trip to Southhampton to spend time with Jessica's family. "What do you say we get married in Southampton? With your family around you?"

Jessica knew why Andrew was suggesting this now. He was anxious to get married and so was she. But he also knew she was worried that she wouldn't have her family around her when they did get married. It was so important to Jessica that she had a part of her mother with her on her wedding day, and the only way she could have that would be for her mother's mother, sisters and brother to be there and witness her joy. And she had been reluctant to reach out to them because she didn't want to be rejected.

And now she would be with them. She had to agree with Andrew that now would be the perfect time to have a small wedding on the beach. It would be cold on the beach, but Jessica didn't care about that. She knew her family probably wouldn't be too thrilled about having a beach wedding in the middle of January, however. But there were ways of making everybody warm. They would build fires on the beach, have heaters on the sand. She had to make sure everything was beautiful and comfortable for everyone, because that was how Jessica was.

"I think that's a great idea," she said to Andrew. "It would be perfect. I'm glad you thought of it."

Andrew kissed her. "I just want to make sure you're happy. And that our wedding will go exactly how you want it. My mother always told me the woman was most important person on anybody's wedding day. Weddings are for the bride, she always said. Maybe that was just her bias, because she was married to my dad."

Jessica smiled. She knew what Andrew was talking about. He was referring to the fact that his father was a very bad person, as he was responsible for the death of Jessica's mother all those years ago. But at least his mother had a beautiful wedding. At least, for one day, she was the queen. She felt beautiful for just that one day. The rest of the marriage was a sham – his father was a violent man with PTSD. Their marriage wasn't happy. But the wedding was wonderful. Whenever she was low, Andrew's mother clung to the feeling that, just for one day, everybody's eyes were on her.

Jessica just shook her head. "Andrew, I love you. Never forget that. But you don't have to spend your entire life trying to make up to me that I have no mother. I think the wedding needs to be about both of us. Our happiness. I have no desire to have everybody look at me and think that I am the most beautiful woman ever, just for the one day. I want everybody to look at us and see our happiness. That's all I want."

Andrew bowed his head. He wanted to protest, Jessica could see, that he was always putting her on a pedestal because he felt responsible for the death of her mother. He had protested that on more than one occasion. At the same time, Jessica knew that what she said was partially true. Andrew was always trying to go out of his way to make Jessica's life as perfect as possible because he felt responsible for her having grown up without a mother. After all, it was his father who killed her mother because his father was aiming for him. There was no getting around that.

But Jessica needed him to know that it was not his responsibility that she be happy. It could never be one person's responsibility for another person's happiness. That wasn't how it worked. Happiness needed to be sought within, not without. And that's what Jessica always thought. So, as much as he meant well whenever he tried to go out of his way to ensure she had more than what she needed in life, she always needed to gently push back. She needed the two of them to be equals, and putting her on a pedestal did not accomplish that.

He finally just nodded. "Okay. We will do our wedding the way both of us want. We will make our wedding about us and not just about the bride."

Jessica smiled and wrapped her arms around the man she loved more than anything in the world. She inhaled the smell of his cologne, felt the warmth of his skin, and felt whole. Before she met Andrew, she never felt like a complete person. She always felt there was something missing, like a vital organ almost. But Andrew filled in that hole.

The two of them planned their trip.

Jessica couldn't be more excited.

Chapter Eight

Ava

Ava heard from Jessica that the two of them, Jessica and Andrew, wanted to be married during their visit to the Hamptons. Ava told everybody that, and everybody got really excited.

And she knew one thing. She needed to invite her friends from California, and Samantha too, out to the Hamptons. They all were a major part of Jessica's life and recovery. Quinn, Hallie, and Sarah all rallied around Jessica and made sure she had everything she needed when she was getting her life together. And her daughter Samantha was a designer of unique wedding cakes. She personally thought her daughter was one of the most talented wedding cake makers she'd ever known.

She wanted to invite everybody, but first had to run it by Jessica and Esther. Jessica obviously would control who would be at her wedding. And Esther invited Ava to stay with her. Esther was her hostess for the month, so she didn't want to put Esther out in any way, shape, or form. Of course, everybody would get their own hotel room. That wasn't a problem, because it was winter time and the hotels all had a lot of vacancies. Still, even if it was just for the weekend, Ava needed to find out if having her friends and daughter around would be an imposition.

Elijah assured Ava it wouldn't be a problem when she brought it up to him. "The more the merrier," he said. "My mother loves to host people at the house. And they wouldn't be around for the whole month. They would only be around for a weekend."

Still, Ava wanted to ensure it would not be a problem.

Of course, when she asked Esther about it, the older woman was more than thrilled. "Of course, of course. If your friends are special to Jessica, then of course they need to be here to see her wedding. That goes without saying."

Jessica was equally excited when Ava asked her about bringing everybody out to Southampton for Jessica's wedding. "Of course, of course!" Jessica shouted over the phone with glee when Ava called her. "I really want the ladies there. I was going to suggest it to my grandmother, but didn't want to put her out. I feel like I'm putting everybody out as it is, just springing a wedding on everybody."

Ava laughed. "Jessica, sweetheart, don't ever think you're putting us out. Trust me, we are all thrilled you're getting your life together and found true love. It is always a cause for celebration when somebody finds her soulmate. It's always a cause for celebration when two people are joined in a union that will never be torn apart. I truly believe that. I believe the two of you were made for each other. That was why you were drawn to one another when you were only small children. It's why the two of you fell in love as adults."

After she cleared it with everybody, it was just a matter of calling the ladies and her daughter to us to ask them to come out. She knew it was short notice, but it wouldn't be a problem with Sarah, because she owned the winery with Ava and they had wine tenders to watch the place whenever they needed time off. Quinn also owned her own business and worked when she wanted. Hallie might be trickier, as she was working at a retreat and often worked weekends. And Samantha, too, might be tricky. She was a cake designer and had a lot on her plate already. She might not be able to just take the time off, even for a couple of days.

So Ava was more than pleased that, when she called everybody, they all anxiously and eagerly accepted. They all said it would be a beautiful thing to see Jessica happy and married.

After she called everybody, she went to the hearth room to tell the Blochs what was going on. But the only person who was in the hearth room at that time was Elijah.

Ava's heart skipped a beat. She wondered if she could ever take a look at her handsome stepbrother without her heart going pitter patter. She swallowed hard. "Good news! It looks like we're going to have a real wedding this weekend."

"A real wedding? As opposed to a fake one?" Elijah said with a sly smile on his face. "That's great. It's so nice my niece is happy after all she went through."

Ava nodded. "Yes. If anybody deserves a happy life, it's her."

Elijah stood up. And then he motioned to a chair. "Have a seat. I'm not really doing much except reading a book."

"What are you reading?"

"A medical thriller. Robin Cook." He smiled. "What can I say, I can't get away from it. But it's nice these books are written by an actual physician. Nothing worse than reading a book written by somebody who clearly doesn't know what they're talking about."

"I know what you mean. I always cringe when I watch legal thrillers, either on the TV or in the movies, and there are things clearly wrong. Like when I watched a show called *How To Get Away With Murder*, and a lawyer questioned witnesses at an appeals hearing. You'd think the show runners would do at least a little bit of research before writing an episode. But they clearly didn't care about getting things right."

Elijah cocked his head. "Questioning witnesses at an appeals hearing? What's wrong with that?"

Ava just chuckled. "There are no witnesses at an appeals hearing. It's just the lawyer arguing his or her case and the judges. The appeals court doesn't look at evidence. They listen to arguments."

Elijah nodded. "You have much experience in appeals?"

"Yeah. I mean not really. I wrote lots of appellate briefs but never argued them in court. I even wrote Supreme Court briefs, a couple of which won the day." Ava found herself really wanting to impress her stepbrother. She figured the best way to do that was to show him that she was not some mooning, silly, middle-school-mentality woman, but a woman of substance. Even though she hated her job as being a lawyer to rich guys trying to evade taxes, she was proud of how well she did it.

"You wrote winning Supreme Court briefs. Impressive."

Ava shrugged. "I guess. I always had a knack for legal arguments and research. Anyhow. That was another life. Another me."

Elijah came over to her and gently brushed her shoulder. "You have a piece of lint on your shoulder," he said.

Ava just held her breath a little as Elijah touched her shoulder.

She finally cleared her throat. "Where is everybody else?"

"Scattered all over the house. It's a big house. And we all try not get in each other's hair too much. If we did, I don't think we would last the entire month. We've always needed our personal space. Except Rachel. She and Valerie were always inseparable."

Elijah looked out the window at the snow that was starting to come down. He hung his head and took a large breath that sounded like a sigh. It was obvious he was still suffering from the loss of his beloved sister.

"Val and Rachel actually wanted to share a room. When Rachel was little, she was afraid of the dark. My mom tried to give her a nightlight, but it did no good. So she asked Valerie if she wanted to share a room with Rachel and she did. So the two of them shared a bedroom throughout their childhood."

"That must've been terrible for her, losing a sister like that. Especially a sister she was really close with."

He nodded. "Something like that happens, the blast radius goes for miles." He shook his head. "Whenever there's a tragedy, the media talks about the victims. The students caught by school shootings. The people burned up in a wildfire. The people killed on 9/11. You know what I'm talking about. The focus should be on the victims, but nobody ever thinks about how many lives each victim touched. Every one of those people you see on the media who lost their lives to tragic circumstances had people who loved them dearly. People who'll never be the same because there's a hole that'll never be plugged. And that's how I feel about Valerie. None of us will ever be the same, least of all

Rachel. And Jessica, of course. Jessica really suffered, because she was there. She saw it happen."

Ava shook her head. "I couldn't imagine something like that. I couldn't imagine losing anybody I loved in such a way." Then she sighed. "Oh, what am I talking about? I lost my husband in that way. The only man I ever loved, Daniel. He was killed in a car accident when I was pregnant with my triplets."

Ava knew what Elijah was talking about when he talked about the blast radius of a tragedy. The blast radius of Daniel's tragedy extended to Ava and her triplets. Her three children grew up without a father because of one stupid decision made by the driver of the car Daniel was in. His friend was three sheets to the wind when he got behind the wheel and ran into a tree, instantly killing himself and Daniel.

Ava sighed. Truth be told, she never really loved again after Daniel. She was infatuated with Deacon for many reasons - his Australian accent, his kindness, his sense of humor and the fact that he was easy on the eyes. But did she love him? Probably not. If she did, she would've been devastated when he moved back to Australia. But she wasn't. She was sad for a little while, but not for long.

But Daniel...she still thought about him just about every day. She loved him dearly. He was the love of her life. Ava was afraid Daniel could never be replaced. Christopher certainly didn't replace him. He stole from her and married somebody else with whom he fathered a child while married to her. However, even if none of that happened, he still wouldn't have been the love of Ava's life. Only Daniel was that for her and maybe that was how it always would be.

Elijah turned to Ava, a haunted look in his big brown eyes. "You never told me that story."

Ava took a deep breath. What was uncovering these feelings? Maybe she was finally ready to move on, 24 years later? She never really had closure. Would she now?

"It's not important," she said. "It was a long time ago."

"You never get over things like that," he said. "Something always brings it back, no matter what. I hate to say it, but having Jessica here will bring it all back to us. Valerie's death. Don't get me wrong, I love my niece. But she is a reminder of all we've lost. But I'm so happy she's getting married. She deserves happiness."

Ava nodded. "Yes, she does. As we all do." Deep breath. "Sometimes I act like I don't deserve happiness. But I can't figure out why I feel that way. I've been a good mother to my kids, a good friend and a good sister. I've just been guarded when it comes to romance. Probably because of Daniel."

"Or maybe it's just that most people our age are guarded in romance. Let's face it, if you get to your mid-50s and you're on your own, it's tough to imagine getting involved with somebody new. You're set in your ways, picky as hell, and probably have a steamer trunk full of emotional baggage. You're looking for just the right puzzle piece and it's not easy to find. So, I can relate."

Ava swallowed hard. Elijah sounded like he was already making excuses for why he didn't want to get involved with somebody, even somebody like herself. "Yeah," Ava said. "I agree with that. But I still have to have a bit of hope. Hope is the only thing that gets me from one day to the next. The hope there's somebody out there who will share my life."

Elijah took a deep breath and then looked out the window again. "Hope it stops soon," he said. "Would suck if we have a wedding in this mess." Then he looked on his phone and nodded. "Good news. This weekend looks clear, with a high of 60 degrees. That's unseasonably warm. So, if we have the wedding in the afternoon, we might not even need the outdoor heaters."

"That would be great," Ava said. "To have it sunny and kind of warm. Warm-adjacent, at any rate."

Just then, Deborah came into the hearth room. "Going into town, any takers?"

"Going with Rachel?" Elijah asked.

"Yeah. She wants to pick up some ingredients for a feast she's planning for the wedding."

Just then, Rachel came into the room as well. "I'm thinking something simple for the wedding," she said. "I really enjoy roasted leg of lamb with Syrian salad, and some fresh green beans with béchamel. And a lovely olive and rosemary loaf of bread." She rubbed her hands together as she looked out the window. "What do you guys think?"

Ava's stomach started to rumble as she thought about the food Rachel was thinking about making. "What is Syrian salad?"

"It's like tabouleh, if you've ever had that," she said. "It has a bulgar wheat base, and it's combined with onion, parsley, olive oil and lemon juice. It goes really well with leg of lamb. And do you know how to make a good béchamel?"

"No,"Ava said. "But I've always wanted to learn."

"How about you help me cook the wedding dinner?" Rachel said. "It sounds like you're interested in learning a few things in the kitchen." She paused. "And béchamel is simple, but not necessarily easy. The classic béchamel is made with whole milk, butter, flour and pepper."

Ava raised an eyebrow. "Sounds like the, um, the shit on a shingle I used to make when I was in college." Ava lived on the veritable shit on a shingle, which consisted of Buddig meat, white bread, and a gravy made with milk, butter, flour and pepper. She never knew that particular gravy had such a fancy French name. She just thought it was a poor college-student meal.

Rachel laughed. "Shit on a shingle. Oh, yeah, I remember that well myself. You're right, the sauce on that particular delicacy enjoyed by poor college students everywhere is a béchamel, come to think of it. But instead of fresh green beans, you put that sauce over Buddig meat and white bread. But you're in the ballpark." She put her arm around Ava. "And the beauty of the béchamel is that it's the basis for many other beautiful sauces, like a Mornay, where you add Swiss cheese to the béchamel."

"Can you teach me to make mayonnaise and Hollandaise?" Ava asked. "I've always wanted to master those two sauces."

"Oh, you're wanting to jump into the deep end, aren't you?" Rachel said. "Well, you're in luck, because Hollandaise will be part of the breakfast on the morning after the wedding. Actually, I was going to make a Béarnaise for the Eggs Benedict. Béarnaise is basically a Hollandaise with vinegar, shallots, tarragon and pepper. So, I'll show you how to make a proper Hollandaise and you can easily turn that into a Béarnaise."

Ava raised an eyebrow. "Eggs Benedict, huh?"

"Yeah," Rachel said. "We're Reformed Jews, so we don't follow all the Kashrut laws. In our case, we won't be eating Canadian Bacon with the Eggs Benedict, but lobster. Lobster Benedicts are the bomb." She nodded her head. "Thank God our family isn't too strict with the Kashrut laws because I love shellfish as much as I love my kids."

Ava noted how nice Rachel was to her, and wondered if her half-sister was trying to make up for being so rude earlier. As much as Ava wanted to trust Rachel, her earlier words still stung. Yes, she apologized, but, at the same time, Ava couldn't help but wonder if Rachel really meant every word but just wasn't supposed to verbalize her thoughts.

Still, she would go along and hope Rachel's sudden friendliness would be the norm from then on. And, truth be told, she was looking forward to learning how to cook basic things from an acclaimed chef who had studied at the same school as Julia Child herself. She always wanted to learn how to make mayonnaise and Hollandaise sauce. She tried to make mayonnaise several times and was never successful. She'd been successful in making mayonnaise with the hand blender but had never been successful in making it in the bowl. You have to add the oil drop by drop and the egg had to be room temperature. She always followed all the instructions to the letter, but she'd never been able to actually make the mayo. As for Hollandaise, she tried to follow the recipes for that sauce, as well, but, as with the mayonnaise, she'd never been able to make it work.

Elijah nudged Ava and gestured to Rachel. "You should go with the girls to town," he said. "There's a lot to see in town, really. Lots of eating places, boutiques, and things like that."

"And we're going to Citarella on the Montauk highway," Rachel said. "It's the gourmet grocer in town."

So, Ava joined Deborah and Rachel in Rachel's Range Rover. The snow was coming down and the streets were icy and slick. Ava wasn't used to this weather anymore, even though she'd lived in New York and Nantucket up until recently.

Deborah turned around in the front seat while Ava sat in the back seat. "We're really happy you're coming with us," Deborah said. "We're going to make this a girl's day. Mom isn't feeling up to coming with us, though. She goes into her treatment tomorrow, so she needs to conserve her energy."

"Oh, a girl's day sounds fun!" Ava said.

"Well, it was Rachel's idea," Deborah said. "To get to know our half-sister, we thought it would be a good thing for the three of us to get out and about."

So, for the rest of the day, Ava, Rachel and Deborah went from one café to another, and shopped at different boutiques. Not everything was open, as it was the off-season, but there were enough places open that it wasn't entirely a ghost town. By the end of it, the three ladies were linking arms as they walked down the sidewalk. Ava and Deborah had been drinking Mimosas and, by the time they got to the gourmet market, Citarella, Ava was feeling buzzed and happy.

Citarella was housed in a wooden structure, and, like most gourmet grocers, it had a perfectly lovely interior. Wood floors and track lighting. The market had everything a foodie would love, and the seafood looked like it was caught that morning.

"Now, your daughter is making the cake, right?" Rachel said, as she pushed her cart and threw herbs, veggies, lemon, sweet potatoes, bulgur, onions, and lamb chops into it. She approached the seafood counter and got 10 lobster tails. In the dairy case, she bought butter, sour cream and whole milk.

"Right," Ava said.

"Well, we still have to have sweets for the breakfast after and a dessert for the wedding dinner," Rachel said. "I'm thinking a nice pear clafouti would be nice for the breakfast, and an apple tart for the wedding dinner."

"What's a pear clafouti?" Ava asked.

"Oh, you'll love it. Poached pears, custard, glazed with homemade apricot jam."

"Custard is another thing I've always wanted to master," Ava said. "It's a basic thing, but I've had it in my head that it's difficult to get right."

"A lot of French cooking is," Rachel said. "Basic ingredients, but the tricky part is in the execution. Stick with me, and you'll go back to Southern California with an entire repertoire of basics. The beauty of mastering the basics is you can add onto them and make all kinds of different things. Like the clafouti. You first have to learn how to make custard, but once you get that down, you can make clafoutis, flan, and créme anglaise."

Rachel approached the pears and examined them. "Anjou pears are the best pears to buy in the wintertime," she said. "They ripen around October but are perfect to buy in January, too."

She picked up several pounds of pears, and headed over to buy the apricot jam. "This place has some of the best jam in the Hamptons."

Ava's mouth watered as she anticipated the lovely dinner and breakfast she would have to look forward to.

"Tonight, we'll be eating Mousse-stuffed fillets of sole," Rachel announced. "White fish, fish mousse, mushrooms and a velouté sauce. A velouté is a bit like a béchamel, but made with heavy cream and Swiss cheese. The fish mousse is made with white fish, heavy cream and egg."

Deborah put her arm around Ava. "See, we told you you'd be eating well on this trip," she said. "You might want to invite Rachel to come live with you just so you can have a personal chef."

"Don't tempt me," Ava said. "I don't eat this well in restaurants."

"Ah, wouldn't I love to live in California," Rachel said. "Naomi needs me, but sometimes I think it would be tough love to let her find her own path."

"Naomi is Rachel's daughter," Deborah told Ava. "She's 23, just out of college, and pretty aimless. She works temp jobs, drives Uber and lives at home. Personally, I think she knows what she's doing by not finding a full-time job. Rachel cooks gourmet meals for her, does her laundry and puts no rules on her whatsoever."

"Well, my fault," Rachel said. "Girl was a women's studies major in college. Which is terrific, if you ask me. But she got that major without a clear goal in mind." Rachel shook her head. "Believe me, you don't get a degree in women's studies if you don't have a clear goal in mind about what you want to do with it. I suggested she get a master's degree in counseling, because that seems to be a logical next step for a women's studies degree. You know, she has a good basis on what women face in today's world, along with the contributions women have made to society. I think she could bring that knowledge into counseling. But she wants to be a musician, of all things." Rachel sighed. "A musician. A singer-songwriter. But she wants to be in a band."

Hmmm….Ava had just finished Duran Duran's John Taylor's memoir. The guy always knew he wanted to be a musician, so he skipped school to pursue his dream. He didn't say as much, but it sounded like he dropped out of school to become a musician in a band. At any rate, he wasn't attending school, so it stood to reason he probably was a high school dropout. But he believed in himself. He knew he was destined for great things. His parents gave him one year to prove himself, and, well, he certainly did. He ate, drank and lived the music scene. Absorbed it in every cell of his body and created some of the greatest music of the early 1980s.

John Taylor, in Ava's mind, was just another example that parents really don't have control of their children. If the kids want to do something passionately enough, they'll do it. And sometimes, as with John Taylor, they rocket to the top. The point was, if a kid is super-passionate about something, they should be supported and nurtured. They wouldn't be forced into something more stable, no matter what their parents say, so, really, in cases of kids who want to go into something artistic, the parents really had two choices - get behind them or be prepared to be cut out of their lives.

Ava nodded. Should she give Rachel advice? She barely knew her half-sister, so who was she to give advice? Then again, she knew from where she spoke. Her kids all chose volatile professions, in a way. Professions where one either sunk or swam. They all were swimming, even Charlotte, who used her art degree to go into ghost-writing novels.

"So, Naomi has no interest in going into counseling. She wants to be a singer-songwriter," Ava said. She took a deep breath. "I hate to say this, but I don't think you'll be successful if you try to force her into getting a master's degree in something she has no interest in. It's best to let her find her way. You know, she has a good basis for songwriting. Having a women's studies degree will help her craft all kinds of feminist songs, and you know those kind of songs tend to be quite popular with a certain segment of the population. Look at Ani DiFranco and Kate Bush. Alanis Morissette. Any number of truly successful women who create songs for other women. Songs about female empowerment, sisterhood and overcoming oppression."

To Ava's surprise, Rachel seemed to absorb Ava's argument without getting upset. She nodded. "You know, I never even thought about that," she said. "I was pretty upset that she got that degree and isn't using it. But I never thought about the angle that the degree might help her write songs. Huh."

Ava smiled. "I know it's tough when your daughter is still living at home, and you're feeling she's not contributing. But it sounds like she needs the space to explore her passion. You're giving her that by allowing her to live at home. But you probably should lay some grounds rules. Like, she needs to be actively pursuing her dream - going to clubs, looking for other people to make up a band, or maybe answering auditions for existing bands. Maybe you could find her somebody like my friend Mia, who not only writes songs but helps others find their song-writing voice."

Rachel raised her eyebrow. "Well, she goes to clubs quite a bit. And open-mic nights and goes to see live music all the time. When she's at home, she's constantly listening to music and making notes in a notebook. She's always practicing her guitar, too, and composing sheet music. I figured she was just spinning her wheels, but maybe I'm wrong."

Deborah nodded. "You see, Rachel, I said the same thing as Ava. Be supportive. You might be surprised about what happens."

"But it's so scary," Rachel said. "To just stand back and hope and pray she doesn't fall on her face. If she can't get lift-off with her music, what will happen to her? I see her living with me for the rest of her life, and that scares me. And what scares me more is that she'll get depressed if she can't make it in the music world."

Ava then told Rachel about her children, especially about Jackson. Jackson struggled mightily in Hollywood and had been since he was 18. He was now 24, and was seemingly on his way. But, for the longest time, Jackson was discouraged and didn't know if he would ever catch a break. That was the reality of pursuing a creative field. It was feast or famine, and the sad reality was that, for most people, it was indeed a famine.

"I understand," Ava said. "Raising kids, in general, is terrifying. We all want what's best for them. The bad thing is, what we feel is best for them is usually quite different than what they think is best for themselves. You just have to close your eyes and hope for the best a lot of times."

Rachel looked resigned. "You're right, Ava," she said. "Anyhow, let's change the subject. Are you excited for the wedding?"

"Oh, yes," Ava said. "Beyond excited."

So, for the rest of the day, the three of them talked like old girlfriends. By the end of their girls' day, Ava felt she knew her half-sisters fairly well.

And Ava made the offer to introduce Naomi to Mia, who had many contacts in the music world. Rachel eagerly agreed to see if Naomi would be game, and called her daughter, who was just as eager to make a new contact.

So Ava felt she did her half-sister some good.

And that made her feel good as well.

Chapter Nine

Jessica

Jessica was apprehensive as she flew into LaGuardia, where she would catch the limousine that Andrew had arranged to take them to her grandmother's house in Southampton. It had been such a long time since she had spoken with anybody in her family, and she wondered how they would treat her. She didn't know how much they knew about her situation. She was frankly ashamed.

Andrew was right next to her on the plane in the limo, holding her hand the entire time. That was one thing about their connection – they really didn't have to speak all the time, but they always knew how the other person was feeling. And there were times when Jessica couldn't quite verbalize how she felt, but Andrew seemed to always know. He was a sensitive artist – a songwriter, a singer, a poet. So he was more sensitive than most guys about how people felt. He also had more empathy for people. That meant he could actually feel what they were feeling, as opposed to just being sympathetic. The upshot was that Jessica always knew she was seen and heard, and that made her feel extremely loved.

So when she was quiet on the flight, and in the limo, Andrew didn't try to make her talk. He just silently held her hand so she knew he was there.

When they were almost to the beach house, Jessica finally spoke about her fears. "I'm really afraid they're going to reject me. I know they asked me to come back here, and they seemed happy about hosting the wedding for us. But I don't know if it's because they feel sorry for me or because they genuinely want to reconnect. I just don't know what to expect."

Andrew nodded silently. "Let's just go into the house and try to feel our way around." Jessica knew that Andrew was really anxious for this reunion to go well. She was just as anxious for it, but at the same time, she was bracing herself for rejection and failure. It was hard for Jessica to feel anything positive when it came to her family. In a way, she felt almost like she was not a part of this family after her mother died. She didn't quite know why that was. Maybe it was because she was a painful reminder of her mother Valerie.

She approached the house, and the first face she saw was Esther. Her grandmother had a big smile on her face and her arms were opened wide. Her grandmother looked frail and had a scarf on her head. But Jessica was so excited that Esther was waiting for her with open arms that she fell into her grandmother's arms and the two embraced or what seemed like 100 years. Esther had tears in her eyes, and then Jessica saw her two aunts and her uncle. Her Aunt Deborah gave her a big hug, Aunt Rachel did the same, and then her Uncle Elijah.

So far so good, Jessica thought. Elijah was taking her

bags up to the spare bedroom, and Esther had her arm around her as they walked into the house.

"How was the trip?" Esther asked eagerly.

"Uneventful, thank God," Jessica said. "Thank you so much for having us and for staging a wedding on such short notice."

"I'm just happy you're happy," Esther said. "I'm an old lady, so I have to admit that I've been thinking about you for all these years, and I wish I would've reached out to you sooner. But you're here now, you're glowing, and nothing makes me happier."

Everybody gathered in front of the fire, and Jessica told everyone about her trip out east. And then she knew she would have to address the elephant in the room. She needed to clear the air, so everybody could just move on.

"I wanted to explain about what's been going on with me for the past few years. I know you all probably thought I was sponging off my grandfather. That I was lazy and didn't want to work. But I've had a lot of problems because I blocked out my mother's death for so long. But it was eating away at me all the same. I didn't really know what happened all these years. I knew my mother was dead, but I didn't really know how she died, even though she was killed right in front of me."

Esther put her hand on Jessica's hand. "Jessica, dear, I had no idea that you had blocked it out. Your father moved away with you for so long, and didn't allow much contact with us. We didn't know what to do. We wanted to stay active in your life, but your father wouldn't allow it. I guess we know now why he wouldn't allow it. He never talked to you about how your mother died?"

Jessica shook her head. "No. He would never discuss it. He was relieved, I guess, that I didn't remember it. I guess he thought that if I didn't remember it, it didn't affect me. But it did affect me. I suffered from crippling depression for most of my life, and then I had a drug addiction. But when I accessed the memories of what happened to my mother, I was able to process it. And when I processed it, it was like a door had opened. It was painful working through that, but I managed to with a lot of therapy. But I'm sorry that my grandfather had to support me for a few years. I don't want any of you to think that I was taking advantage of an old man. I loved my grandfather. He was very generous."

Deborah put her arm around Jessica. "We failed you. There is no other way of putting it. As Mom said, we should've been more active in your life all along. Maybe if we were, we could have helped you a long time ago."

Jessica nodded. "Well, I learned through therapy that you need to start fresh with people. That you can't dwell on the past. There is no way of changing the past, so you can't even try. The only thing you can do is go forward with an open heart and open mind. And not to let resentments fester. And that regrets only do one beneficial thing – they help you become a better person because you don't want to repeat the thing that made you regret. But regrets can be corrosive, because they're always going through your head like a loop. They'll pop up at the worst time and they really do a number on your psyche and your self-esteem. So if the regrets are not used to better yourself, they're best left in the past."

Rachel took a deep breath. "I guess what you're saying is that we all regret not being closer to you over the years. But those regrets are not healthy unless they are used to motivate us to pursue a much closer relationship with you in the future."

"Exactly," Jessica said. "Regrets are healthy if they are

used to motivate. They're unhealthy if they're just used to beat yourself up about your failings."

Jessica had been through years of therapy, so she learned a lot. And she was going to take what she learned and apply it to her relationship with her family. She would approach all of them with a fresh heart and knew that was the best way for them to heal their rift.

Chapter Ten

Ava

Jessica arrived that Friday morning with Andrew in tow. She was giddy, and looked positively glowing, Ava thought. Ava thought wistfully about being young like Jessica and madly in love. She thought about why she was being so sentimental about love and marriage these days. She felt she was edging ever closer to getting her own happy ending. It was right around the corner, it seemed, yet it also seemed completely out of reach.

She had a wonderful time with Rachel learning all the new cooking techniques that she always wanted to master and never could. She even made mayonnaise successfully for the very first time in her life. It turned out very well, to her surprise. It was painstaking work, and demanded much patience, but it was worth it in the end to have a lovely aioli that she could be proud of. And making hollandaise for the first time successfully was a revelation. She imagined herself holding brunches for her ladies featuring homemade Eggs

Benedict. She also imagined putting hollandaise on just about everything. She was going to go crazy in the kitchen when she got home because of the techniques Rachel had taught her.

The wedding would be the next day. As Elijah said, the high was going to be 60°, which was positively balmy for this time of year in the Hamptons. Nevertheless, the beach would have to be set up with fire rings and heaters. Esther arranged for all of that, and workers were busily setting everything up for the small and intimate wedding that would happen the very next day.

Her ladies arrived later on Friday, along with her daughter, Samantha, Quinn's daughter Emerson and Sarah's daughter Julia. Andrew's mother also came on short notice, and everyone was busy getting to know her. Also, Quinn's love Mia arrived with Quinn and Conrad arrived with Hallie. Ava was pleased to see Conrad had accompanied Hallie to the Hamptons. Hallie and Conrad were holding hands and staring at each other the entire time. It really seemed the two of them were made for each other. So, Quinn was madly in love with Mia. Hallie and Conrad seemed to be just as much in love as Mia and Quinn. Ava was over the moon for both of her friends who seemed to find their soul mates. Not to mention Samantha, who was still blissfully in love with her best friend turned romantic partner, Grayson.

Sarah was still single. Ava knew that was definitely Sarah's choice. Sarah was drop dead gorgeous and sweet. She was intelligent and worldly. She could have any man she wanted, but she apparently didn't want a man. She was happy raising Julia on her own and working at the winery. Ava knew Sarah was still gun shy. Her long time boyfriend, Nolan, was terrible to her. He was controlling and did something unforgivable when he wrote a letter to the architectural licensing agency in California, stating lies about Sarah selling drugs to children, because he wanted Sarah to lose her license so he could control her. Nolan died and Sarah did not mourn him. Then she fell in love with Max, Julia's father, who died shortly after they were married.

With the kind of luck Sarah had with relationships, Ava wasn't surprised that Sarah didn't want to venture into a new relationship anytime soon.

Everybody gathered at a nearby seafood restaurant that evening, and Jessica was the toast of that gathering. Everybody was excited for Jessica, and Ava was thrilled to see Jessica enjoying hugs and smiles with her family. Maybe the family was wrong in not being more supportive of Jessica, even if they didn't know about her drug problem, but that seemed to be water under the bridge at the moment.

Ava was looking forward to seeing Jessica taking her vows.

And she knew Jessica felt the same.

Chapter Eleven

Jessica

Jessica was so happy when she walked down to the beach in the white dress she'd purchased in Los Angeles from a vintage store. It couldn't be more perfect. It was 2 o'clock in the afternoon, and the weather was clear and cool. It was so cool that they definitely had to make use of the outdoor heaters that were set up around the makeshift altar, and about twenty feet away, a bonfire burned.

Esther managed to get a nondenominational reverend to do the honors for the two of them. Jessica did not consider herself to be religious, and neither did Andrew. Her mother was Jewish, but her father was not religious. Since her father bought her up, not her mother, Jessica, too, was without a religion. She was absolutely thrilled that it all came together in such a short period of time. And she was over the moon as she took her vows with the man she had loved since she was a very young girl. Like Andrew, she knew when she was four years old that she met her soul-mate. And now, here it was, over 20 years later, and she was marrying the little boy she met on Nantucket all those years ago.

The fact that that little boy grew up into an international pop superstar didn't matter to Jessica. What mattered to her was that he was hers, and would be forever.

The dinner that was served after the ceremony was phenomenal. Tender leg of lamb served with a light grain salad with red onions, tomatoes, cucumbers, and parsley. It was light and delicious, and just what Jessica wanted for her ceremony. It was simple yet phenomenally tasty and healthy. The apple tart that came afterward was just as phenomenally delicious, heavy on the cinnamon and brown sugar, all surrounded by a light and flaky crust.

All in all, Jessica thought it was the perfect wedding. Light on the fuss and the pomp, heavy on the bonding and conversation with her family and friends surrounding her.

And, if she wasn't mistaken, she saw a connection between Ava and Elijah. They sat next to one another, and their banter and conversation was just so easy between the two of them. Ava looked positively glowing as she sipped her champagne and laughed hysterically at things Elijah was whispering in her ear. Elijah, for his part, had a similar glow on his face. He lightly put his arm around Ava while he talked to his sister Deborah, who was on his right. It was almost like he didn't quite realize what he was doing, having his arm around Ava, like it was an unconscious thing he just couldn't help.

Jessica smiled. She knew just by looking at Ava and Elijah that the two of them were meant for one another. She wondered if Elijah and Ava realized their feelings for one another. Jessica was bathed in love, both the love of her new husband Andrew and the newfound love of her family.

She was so happy and wanted everybody else to be just as happy. She knew from talking to Deborah and Rachel that her aunts were both divorced from really awful men. And they were having problems with their children. Jessica felt for both of them. She wanted to find somebody for her aunts as well, but, at the moment, she didn't really know who they could be matched up with.

But Ava? She definitely had her love and he was sitting right next to her. Jessica would have to have a talk with Ava about that in private.

Ava stood up to give the toast, since Ava was one who knew her best.

"Jessica, what can I say except I cannot be prouder that you have come such a long way and have found lasting love. I still think about when you came to my door a few years ago. You were lost and alone and at the end of your rope. You were fighting hard for your survival, and you came to work for me. And you worked harder than anybody I had ever seen. But there was always something missing in your life. Then you found out the root of your distress, got the necessary therapy, got help for your substance abuse, and used your inner strength to overcome. And now, here you are, sober, working on your master's degree, and married to the man of your dreams. You did all of that. It was all down to your tenacity and faith in yourself. You didn't let your experiences break you, but they made you stronger. And I know that you and Andrew will go the distance because you were made for one another. Cheers, Jessica and Andrew."

"L'Chaim," Esther said as everybody raised their glass. L'Chaim was Hebrew for "to life."

"L'Chaim," everybody repeated.

Jessica sipped sparkling grape juice while everybody else

drank champagne, and that was okay. She loved sparkling grape juice.

After the ceremony and the dinner, everybody headed down to the beach and sat around a bonfire. They laughed, joked, and told stories until well into the night.

And Jessica was in such a happy mood that she decided to take Ava aside to tell her feelings about Ava and Elijah.

" Ava," Jessica said. "What don't you and I go get our winter coats, and take a walk along the beach? It's a beautiful evening, a full moon, and the waves are just perfect."

Ava nodded, and Elijah volunteered to go back to the house and get Jessica and Ava a stocking cap and winter coat. Elijah returned 10 minutes later with the provisions in hand, and Ava and Jessica bundled up and left the bonfire party to take a walk along the shore.

Ava put her arm around Jessica as the two walked next to the oncoming waves. "I'm so proud of you," she said.

"I couldn't have done it without you," Jessica said. "When I came to your house that day, I was on the verge of killing myself. Literally. I was homeless, depressed, addicted, and had zero hope for the future. If you didn't take me in, I probably would have drowned myself in the ocean, and that's no lie. That's what I was planning on doing that day."

Ava nodded. "That doesn't surprise me. But I knew. I saw a light in your eyes when you came to my door, so I knew you were a fighter and a survivor. And you had a great capacity to love."

"As do you. Have a capacity to love. You're wonderful to everybody around you. But I wanted you to know that I see something between you and Elijah. I was wondering if you ever thought about the two of you getting together?"

Ava cleared her throat. "How did you know?"

"It's obvious to anybody who's looking. And, I don't know, maybe I'm more sensitive to your nonverbal cues because I know you so well."

Ava shook her head. "I don't think he feels the same."

"Oh, but he does. He does. I can see it in his eyes the same way I can see it in yours. It's in the way he looks at you, the way he gestures towards you, the way the two of you seem to have your own language. I look at the two of you and I see two people who are completely in sync, comfortable with one another and have an easy rapport. Who are in love with one another, even if they don't want to admit it just yet."

Ava stopped walking. "Do you really think that?"

"I know it. Maybe it'll be a little strange because you both have the same half-sisters, but as long as there's no parents in common, there is nothing weird or wrong about falling in love with Elijah. I want you to be happy. I'm happy because of you. So I want you to find the same degree of happiness."

Ava didn't say anything. The two of them walked silently back to the group huddled around the bonfire.

Perhaps it was a good thing that Ava didn't say anything.

At least she didn't protest.

Chapter Twelve

Ava

The month at Southampton went way too quickly. Ava absolutely loved staying with Esther and her two half-sisters Deborah and Rachel, and, of course, Elijah. She really got to know Deborah and Rachel and grew to love both of them. She was surprised how close she and Rachel grew over the month, as Ava became a veritable sous chef to her half-sister. She chopped vegetables for Rachel, deboned chickens – before she came on this vacation, she couldn't hardly chop up the chicken, let alone debone it - and learned everything she could about making stews, sauces, soups, game, meat, fish and roasted vegetables. She felt she had a crash course in cooking, learning at the right hand of a world-class chef. So she definitely considered her vacation to be a productive one.

As for Esther, she completed her chemotherapy treatments and was given a clean bill of health at the last visit to her doctor. So, as it turned out, this was not a last goodbye at all. In fact, Ava thought that Esther would live to be over 100 years old and end up line dancing with twentysomethings at wedding receptions just like Ava saw on that viral YouTube video.

But the only thing was, she still didn't tell Elijah how she felt about him. Yes, Jessica encouraged her to verbalize her feelings. And she took it to heart, their walk and talk along the beach that night. Yet, something always stopped her when she really wanted to open her mouth to say something to him.

But the two of them were traveling together back to Southern California. And, once they got back there, they were a part of each other's lives. That had always been the case. Ever since Ava met Elijah, the two of them met often for coffee, dinner, and Shabbat on the beach. So, it wasn't like they would go back to Southern California and just disappear from one another's lives.

On the last day of her vacation, Ava sat in her room, opened up the windows and listened to the surf roll in. It was early February, so was still quite cold and snow was still on the beach. The town was still quiet, the tourists not being due for another several months. She thought about what she would have to do when she got back. Sarah had been manning the winery, with the help of their young wine tenders, and was doing a spectacular job of it, but Ava would have to return to the winery in full force when she arrived back in Los Angeles.

Ava loved her winery and missed it dearly. She really enjoyed holding events there, but also really loved bantering with everyday customers. They hadn't yet held any tours of the place - they would wait until harvest season for that - but there was something about having a rapport with happy people that cheered Ava immensely. And people at her winery usually were happy, Ava thought. That was the whole point of going to a winery - to have fun with your friends or significant other. People didn't go to wineries to drown their sorrows as they would in a bar. They came to have a good time.

So, she looked forward to getting back to that. And she looked forward to getting back to the ritual of hanging out with her ladies.

But she didn't look forward to living alone again. Here in this Hampton's house, she was part of a fabric. People under this roof loved one another, occasionally fought, but definitely were bonded. Ava was a part of their game nights, movie nights, dinners, lunches, brunches, breakfasts. She was a part of their late-night bonfires, evenings around the hearth-room fireplace drinking wine and contemplating the meaning of life. She was a part of Rachel's cooking, and Deborah's photography - she went out with Deborah on many different occasions to shoot sunrises on the beach, animals in the forest, the desolate downtown landscape at dawn. She hadn't experienced this level of closeness since her college days, and knew she'd miss it dearly.

Most of all, though, she'd miss being around Elijah every day.

Just then, Elijah popped his head through her open door. "You packing?" he asked, his hands stuck in his pockets.

Ava nodded silently, suddenly on the verge of tears. "Yes," she finally said as she went to her armoire and got some more clothes out of it. "I always hate saying goodbye. You know, that's the worst thing about vacations. They end and you have to go back to your life. I inevitably experience a post-vacation letdown at the end of any vacation. It's almost not worth going on vacation."

Elijah smiled. "Know what you mean. You're in a bit of a fantasy world when you're on vacation. Nothing is real. Then you get thrown back unceremoniously into your life and it's jarring for a day or two."

Ava smiled. He understood her. He didn't try to minimize her depression about going back, didn't try to tell her she was silly or whining about first-world problems. He understood her way more than Christopher ever did. Daniel had understood her in this way, Ava thought. She could tell Daniel anything and would know her husband got it. Christopher always tried to tell Ava her feelings were wrong, but Daniel never did.

Elijah was much like Daniel in that regard.

"You mean this isn't the real world?" Ava joked, her eyes wide.

Elijah chuckled. "If only it were. No, I take that back. It's a part of life, vacation. Everybody needs it to recharge their batteries. But I think that if I had to live my life like this - just hanging about, drinking wine and playing Scrabble - I would be in the loony bin within a few months. My life has to have a purpose."

"Yes," Ava agreed, although she didn't know exactly what was the purpose in her life. Making people happy at her winery was a good purpose, she supposed, but she wasn't saving lives every day like Elijah was.

Stop Ava. Stop that negative voice comparing yourself to Elijah. Yes, you aren't saving lives, but making people happy at the winery isn't nothing.

Ava smiled as her internal monologue continued apace.

The two of them sat down on the bed. Ava put her head on his shoulder and he put his arm around her.

And then, something came over her.

She turned to Elijah and looked into his soulful brown

eyes. "Elijah, I love you." Her breathing was coming faster and faster. *Well done, Ava. Now you're either going to be embarrassed to fly back with him and too ashamed to see him in Los Angeles or you're going to be the happiest woman in the world.*

But Elijah didn't get it. "I love you too," he said, but Ava thought he was just telling her that he loved her like the step-sister she really was to him.

Gut check time. "No, I mean I love you. As in, giving-you-the-last-delectable-fudge-brownie, not-say-anything-when-you-leave-up-the-toilet-seat love you. I want to be with you."

She hung her head, but Elijah took her chin in his hand and looked into her eyes. "I thought you'd never say it." Then he kissed her and she completely lost herself. She felt that kiss to her very marrow, like she was kissing somebody she'd known forever yet who excited her like nobody ever had before. Even Daniel. It was just how she thought it would be, kissing him.

And then he looked at her. "Are we doing this, you and me? Because, I'll be honest, I've thought of little else since I've met you."

So Jessica was right, Ava thought. Jessica told her that Elijah loved her as much as she loved him. She saw the love in Ava and Elijah's eyes the night of the wedding dinner. How could she have missed the cues all this time?

She finally nodded. "I'd like to really do this. Because I've thought of little else since I met you."

He smiled and ran his fingers through her hair and kissed her again. "It's just like I thought it would be, kissing you," he said. "Oh, how I've wanted to do this for months and months."

Ava swallowed hard. She was finally getting her wish. All this time, she thought she was perfectly content with her life. She had her best friends, her children, her winery, her sister. A full and happy life. Then she met Elijah and completely re-evaluated what she really wanted. And she was, finally, ready to move on from Daniel. Ready to put Daniel into the sacred space of memories, not to be dwelled upon and mourned but to be celebrated. Daniel would've wanted this for her, to finally love again. She knew this, because that was how Daniel was - selfless, giving, wanting the best for Ava.

Ava's heart started to skip as she realized that she had finally found the man to help her truly move on. She didn't want to question it. Didn't want to ruin the mood by asking him if he was okay dating somebody who had the same half-sisters he did. No, she wasn't going to question any of it. She was just going to go with her heart.

And her head. Because Deborah was right - the brain must also be involved in a romantic decision. And Ava's brain was as stimulated by the handsome Elijah as her heart was.

Ava closed her eyes and listened to the sounds of her breath and Elijah's pounding heart. Yes, this was happening. It was obvious now to Ava that they both desperately wanted it to happen.

A few minutes later, they were in bed together, making love with the tender passion Ava had never experienced in her life.

She finally belonged to somebody.

And she was over the moon.

Next in the Sconset Beach Series

vinci-books.com/beachfront-winery

Love, loss and second chances at a beachfront winery.

As Sarah yearns for her own happily ever after, she finds herself drawn to the captivating art dealer, Silas Pierce. Their shared passions ignite a deep connection, but a dark secret from Silas's past threatens to shatter Sarah's newfound happiness. Will she finally find the love she deserves, or will Silas's secret upend her dreams once more?

Turn the page for a free preview…

The Beachfront Winery: Chapter One

Sarah

Ava was back in town, and was happier than Sarah had ever seen her. Ever. She was positively glowing as she served the various customers who came in to sample wine and buy bottles from the Sava winery. She was beaming as she talked to some of the regulars, including Joe, a firefighter who came into the winery all the time with his buddies, and Jean, a middle-aged woman who loved to bring her lady friends for some wine-tasting and lectures about all the latest wines Sava was offering.

Sarah knew why Ava was so darned happy - she was finally in love with a man who was not only her equal, but her age. As lovely as Ava's last love interest, Deacon, was, it just wasn't in the cards because of the age difference. Before Deacon, it was Christopher, the jerk who stole all Ava's money before coming back around and trying again. Ava kicked him to the curb for good after he confessed to having another family while he was married to her. The nerve of some people, Sarah thought, shaking her head.

While Sarah was thrilled for her sister, she suddenly realized that she was the only one of her friend group who was unattached. Mia and Quinn were going strong, as were Hallie and Conrad. Fiona, who was Sarah's new friend, was very happy with Jack. And now Ava was blissfully in love with Elijah, her step-brother-turned-soul-mate. Even Jessica, who was Ava's niece and one-time protegée, was married to Andrew, the pop-star who Jessica knew as a child and loved as an adult.

Love was all around her and she wondered if Cupid would hit her next. Not that Sarah was necessarily anxious for that. She had a wonderful life raising Julia and running the winery with Ava. She lived with Quinn and her daughter, Emerson, so she was never lonely in the evenings. Quinn and Mia were both great fun to hang with, as they often did in the evening, watching old movies on TCM, grabbing sushi from the restaurant down the street, going to the beach and watching the waves. But Sarah was starting to feel like a third wheel with Quinn and Mia, and she now had nobody single to run around with. And that felt a bit… strange.

She never imagined, when she was in high school and was the golden girl, the homecoming queen, the trendsetter, the girl who everybody looked up to and had boys falling at her feet, that she would get to the age of 54 with nothing but a broken heart to show for her romantic endeavors. She hated Nolan, the man who beat her down for years and years and made her afraid to love again. She fell in love with Max, but he was dying, which, Sarah had to admit, was a part of why she allowed herself to love him. It was a love with an expiration date, which meant she didn't have to truly commit to him. As painful as that was to admit, Sarah was still so terrified of committing to somebody that she could only become attached to a dying man.

She knew why. Nolan seemed perfect when she met him. Handsome, wealthy, worldly and seemingly kind, he swept Sarah off her feet. Sarah didn't even think about the moves she made after meeting him - quitting her job to follow him around, leaving her entire architectural career in the dustbin. The architectural career that she worked so hard for, getting a master's from Stanford and a bachelor's at the University of Missouri, was forgotten like a Craig's List free couch left by the side of the road. She had to quit because Nolan required his paramour to be free to travel the world and Sarah had always nursed a serious case of wanderlust. She didn't think twice about walking away from her first love, architecture, to indulge in her second love, travel.

And when it all inevitably fell apart after Sarah took the rap for her "friend" Lauren's drugs and Nolan sealed her fate by writing a letter to the California Architects Board filled with lies about her selling drugs to children, Sarah was stuck in a life with a man she now despised but had grown reliant upon because her career was well and truly dead. She thought that would be her entire life, following around a man she hated but who took care of her, but Nolan died a terrible death after suffering from ALS for several years and Sarah was free.

She didn't grieve.

She felt relieved.

Thank God Nolan passed away, Sarah thought with only a small amount of guilt. If he didn't, Sarah would've still been his prisoner. But she wasn't. She was living her best life with friends she loved. But, at the same time, her fear of getting involved with another man who would treat her like a possession to control kept her from looking at anybody of the opposite sex with any degree of romantic interest.

That day, she was busy waiting and bussing tables and selling their wines. Sarah was a wine expert, as she traveled the world, sampling wine wherever she sent. It was a warm day in the middle of March, and spring was definitely in the air. Sarah loved the autumn and winter, loved the shorter days, the crispness in the air and the changing leaves, even though not every tree lost its foliage in Los Angeles during the wintertime. It made her just a bit sad when the winter was over and spring was upon them, but, at the same time, she was looking forward to tending her garden and growing roses, tomatoes, cucumbers and other flowering plants.

Nevertheless, Sarah somehow dreaded the coming of spring because it meant an end to the seasons she always loved. But, on the bright side, business certainly picked up with the warmer weather. March wasn't the warmest month in Los Angeles, not even close, but it was starting to warm up just a bit and people started to get spring fever. She noticed the outdoor dining was picking up all over Venice Beach, and her winery was seeing the spillover. And it would soon be June, the time of weddings and love. Sarah knew her winery would really start to jam during that busy season.

Sarah went over to a table where a well-dressed man was sitting. He was elegantly dressed in a silk beige shirt and light brown dress pants, no tie, with the top buttons undone, showing just a hint of chest hair. His dark tightly curled hair was cut close on the sides, long on top, and he was wearing a Rolex on his right wrist. He held a phone in his left hand and was talking rapidly in Mandarin Chinese, a language Sarah knew as well. The man was incredibly handsome, with green eyes, long eyelashes, a straight nose and bow-shaped lips.

Sarah got a whiff of the man's cologne, the heady scent she recognized as Aventus Creed, a top-drawer cologne featuring bergamot, black currant, patchouli, rose and and oak, amongst other tempting olfactory delights. She shook her head, feeling a draw to this handsome man unlike anything she'd felt for a long time, maybe ever.

Then he smiled at her, his clear green eyes shining, his straight teeth framed by full lips, and Sarah felt that smile like a beam of light. She involuntarily put her hand to her heart and felt it thumping beneath her fingers. She blinked and opened her mouth to ask for his order, but nothing came out.

"Hey," he said, his voice like thick, deep honey. "I'd like a bottle of your best Cabernet Sauvignon." He pointed to the menu at the bottle that Sarah and Ava sold for $500. "I'm waiting on some friends, so I need three glasses." Then he smiled again, and Sarah lost her breath.

Damn, that was a weird reaction for her. When she met Nolan, it was a different reaction than what she just experienced with this mystery man. She fell for Nolan because he was a gentleman at first, giving her a ride home when she needed it after being caught in the rain. She got to know him gradually, liking his mind and his manners. As for Max, she hated him at first because he accused her of being some kind of flaming liberal just because she didn't want to ban the same books he did, or, to be exact, didn't want to ban books at all. That she fell in love with Max came to an absolute surprise to her, not to mention surprising her friends.

But she'd never before experienced the kind of heart-pounding, lights-shining-from-above type of lightning bolt she just felt as she looked at this mystery man. Fiona, who was the resident matchmaker of Venice Beach, would no-doubt tell Sarah that she just met her soul-mate and that was why she had that reaction to the man. Sarah didn't necessarily believe in soul mates, the notion that souls travel throughout time and find one another again and again. But maybe she was wrong about that.

Sarah just nodded and wanted to ask if the friends he was expecting were male or female, but felt too nervous to ask that question. And she didn't want to be obvious about it. "I'll be right back out with that wine," she managed to croak out. "Can I interest you in any appetizers?"

He nodded. "Yes, a charcuterie plate would be nice," he said. "The one with the olives, brie, sun-dried tomatoes and fruit." He nodded. "That sounds like it would go well with the cab."

"It does," Sarah said with a smile. "That's my favorite charcuterie plate, actually."

At that, she walked back to the wine-tasting room where Ava was busy pouring more wine and chatting up several of the regulars who were getting drunk off Pinot Grigio and eating chicken wings. Ava smiled as Sarah came in. "Hey, sis, what can I get you?"

"The top-shelf cab," Sarah said.

"Oooo," Ava said. "I thought we'd never sell that bottle. Who's the high-roller?"

"A guy," Sarah said. "He's sitting outside, waiting on a friend."

Ava cocked her head. "Hmmm," she said as she studied Sarah's face. "You like this guy, don't you?"

Was she that transparent? Yes, she probably was. After all, Ava was her sister. Her sister was going to know when something was up.

She put her hands to her cheeks. "Yes," she admitted. "I

don't know, something happened when I saw this guy. I know nothing about him, other than the facts that he is incredibly handsome, dresses impeccably and smells delicious. And he has a voice like thick honey. If the man isn't a DJ at a smooth jazz station, he's missed his calling. But, other than that, I know nothing about him, but feel like I know him very well. Weird."

Ava nodded. "Sounds like Cupid finally found you," she said.

"Oh, come on," Sarah said. "I just said I don't know this man. That means I have no idea if he's any good. But he speaks fluent Mandarin Chinese, so it's safe to say he has some level of education because he's clearly not Chinese."

Ava grinned as she handed Sarah the bottle of Cab and the wine bottle opener. "Say what you want, but I think you've been hit by lightning. Finally. All my life, I've been wanting to see you hit by lightning and you never were. Lots of guys saw you and felt hit by lightning, but never the other way around."

Sarah knew that was true. She was always the heartbreaker, at least until Nolan, where she found herself the heartbroken. And she didn't like it. She didn't like it one bit. That said, Ava was right. There were many men along the way who told her she was The One. Men who Sarah thought in her mind were good for a short period, nothing more.

And Ava was also correct in saying that Sarah had never really fell for anybody before. Then again, she'd never met anybody who lit a spark for her the way this mystery man did just now.

She took the bottle of Cab and the charcuterie plate out to the man, who was now joined by two other people. They were all laughing and talking and the sound of this man's laughter lit Sarah up from within.

Sarah smiled, opened the bottle of wine, gave the cork to the man and poured a small amount into a glass for him to sip and give the okay for the bottle of wine. The man smelled the cork, took a sip, and smiled. "That's the stuff. That's what I'm talking about." Then he raised his hand for Sarah to shake. "My name is Silas Pierce. And who is serving this magnificent bottle of wine?"

"Sarah Flynn," Sarah said. "And, as you might have guessed, the bottle of wine you're enjoying is not one of our vintage. We've only been bottling wine for about a year, and this particular bottle is a 1984 vintage. That year was one of the best in the area in recent memory."

Silas nodded. "Yes, 1984 was a great year in this area for wine. The wines for that year were unusually robust, fruity, complex and rich. This bottle of wine is the perfect example of that."

At that, Sarah poured a glass for Silas' two companions, who both took a sip and nodded. "Delicious," the woman to his left said, swirling the burgundy liquid around in her glass. "Probably the smoothest glass I've ever had."

The guy to his right agreed. Sarah smiled and said she would be back to check on them. The group heartily said they would be looking forward to that.

Sarah went back into the tasting room and put her tray on the bar. "There's a woman with him," Sarah said dejectedly.

"And?" Ava asked.

"And nothing. I just wanted to state a fact." Sarah sighed. "Let's face it, the only men who will be available at this age will be carrying a lot of baggage or already would be in a happy relationship. Seems I missed my window for when that wouldn't be the case."

Ava laughed. "And what window was that?"

"You know, back in the day when everything was fresh and new and everybody didn't have 18 million exes and hadn't had their heart broken a bazillion times."

"And when was that?" Ava asked, clearly amused.

"I don't know. When we were 10, I guess."

"Exactly,"Ava said. "Let's face it, if you are a normal person, your heart gets broken a million times by the time you're 13. Maybe even younger. Not to mention, when you're young like that, you have a lot of other emotional issues that have nothing to do with the opposite sex and what they did to you. Maybe you don't remember it, but being young isn't always fun. You have so many pressures, you're not comfortable in your skin, so many insecurities, and high school is kind of a chaotic time. Personally, I think the best time is now. We are comfortable in our skin, we have money of our own, we have developed talents, and we're less likely to put up with bullshit."

Sarah knew exactly what Ava was talking about. While she was definitely one of the most popular girls in school, if not the most popular, it didn't mean she didn't have a ton of pressure on her. She did. She was constantly worried that people were going to talk about her behind her back, constantly worried she would fail somehow, and her failure would be so much more magnified than if she wasn't so well-known and well-liked in school. Worse than that, she never thought much of herself and never quite knew exactly what was expected of her. Everybody saw her as the golden girl, the head cheerleader, the school leader, the homecoming queen. All Sarah saw when she looked in the mirror was a girl who didn't measure up, who wasn't good enough, who wasn't worthy of all the attention. She had the worst case of imposter syndrome ever, but nobody ever knew this about her. She somehow managed to fake her way through school, acting the part of the girl who everybody thought she was, while secretly thinking she was a nobody.

Of course, she never told Ava this. Ava, at that time, would've rightly told her to quit whining. She had everything the awkward Ava ever wanted, so what problems did she have? Plenty, as it turned out, and she was never happy.

But now she was happy. Insanely so. Ava was right - it took time and maturity, but, like that beautiful bottle of wine she served up to Silas and his friends, the time and maturity made her finally feel beautiful and worthy, even though, in her mind, she clearly wasn't as physically beautiful as she was when she was 16. But her feeling beautiful was just a mind-set, and she would've had that same mind-set if she weren't objectively beautiful but quirky and strange, like she really wished she always had been.

Her feeling beautiful came from feeling happy and content, not by looking at a flawless face in the mirror. And that feeling was so much better than having everybody tell her how gorgeous she was when she felt anything but.

"You know, Ava, you're right. I'm really in a better place in my life to have a healthy relationship than I was when I was young and dumb and thought I knew everything. Thanks for making me see that."

Ava nodded. "Sis, you know that's what I'm here for. I'm always here to show you reality. And, in this case, reality is better than what you're thinking in your head. You have a lot to offer anybody, Sarah. You know this now more than you ever have before. So go forth in confidence that you will enrich anybody's life."

Sarah sighed. "Thanks for the shot in the arm. Now, to

subtly find out if Silas just happens to be single and ready to mingle."

"Mystery man's name is Silas?" Ava asked. "What a cool name. You don't hear that name very often, but it's really an amazing one. What does it mean, do you know?"

Sarah looked it up quickly. "Of the forest," Sarah said. "It's Greek." Sarah breathed heavily. "Of the forest." She closed her eyes, thinking of all the times she visited forests and the peaceful times she felt during these trips. The smells of leaves, pine and wet grass and the sounds of owls, crickets, frogs, streams and the wind rustling through the trees were peaceful to Sarah. How fitting that this man with the placid green eyes and golden skin had a name that echoed the forest.

"Silas Pierce," Sarah said, "is his first and last name."

Ava raised an eyebrow. "He's got a great name, I'll give him that."

"A great name for a sexy and handsome man," Sarah said dreamily. "Anyhow, I need to get to work. As do you." Sarah motioned to a group of 20-somethings who were coming through the door.

As Sarah was leaving the wine-tasting room, she bumped into Silas, who was coming in. She smiled and looked down at the floor. "You looking for the restroom?" she asked.

"No, actually. I was looking for you."

Sarah nodded. "I was just coming out to check on you guys. Is there something I could get for you?"

He walked over the bar and leaned on it and put one of his fingers up to his temple as he casually smiled at Sarah. "Yeah," he said slowly. "There is, as a matter of fact. I'd like your business card. I need a good sommelier who knows her stuff because I do a lot of entertaining and it's always a good thing to have the digits of a beautiful woman who knows her way around a bottle of wine."

Sarah nodded and went over to the bar, behind which she kept her cards. Then she casually wrote her cell number on the back. "My cell," she said. "You know, just in case you need an emergency bottle of wine for a fund-raiser or casual dinner with friends."

Silas smiled, his teeth brilliant and white. "You know, Sarah Flynn, I just might call this cell." He raised an eyebrow. "You know, maybe there's a casual dinner with a certain beautiful sommelier in the works. You never know."

Sarah felt herself blush. "Are you making an offer?"

"I am," he said, his voice sounding like buttery caramel. "You interested?"

Sarah nodded. "What did you have in mind?"

"What about dinner tomorrow night. Short notice, I know, but I have to fly out to China on the weekend and I'll be there for 10 days. But I don't like the grass to grow under my feet, so I thought I'd take a chance."

Sarah thought back to Silas' conversation in fluent Mandarin Chinese when she first came upon him. "China, huh?" Sarah had been to China multiple times herself, not just to the usual touristy haunts like Beijing and Shanghai, but also the small villages and rural areas where most tourists never dare venture.

"Yes," he said. "I'm an independent curator for art galleries around the city, and I'm working with LACMA right now on a contract basis. It's expanding their Asian art collection. I have some meetings with some museums in Beijing, as we're doing an exchange with them and they're offering several priceless paintings and sculptures on loan." "LACMA" referred to the Los Angeles County Museum of

Art, which housed one of the largest Asian art collections in the area.

Sarah put her hand to her heart. This man seemed too good to be true, at least on the surface. He undoubtedly had a PhD in art history or a similar area, so he had the intelligence, culture and education that Sarah craved in any man. He was also undoubtedly worldly, if he was a curator for the largest art museum in the area. That meant he and Sarah had travel and worldliness in common, and he was probably as curious as she was about the different peoples in the world.

Sarah took a deep breath. She didn't want to seem eager to have dinner with him, because a part of her still enjoyed the feeling of being chased. Yet, she knew she had to act fast, or this guy would be gone for 10 days and might not be back in to see her if she delayed him. And, unfortunately, the next evening was her turn to work late. But Ava probably would be more than willing to pick up Sarah's shift if Sarah asked her really nicely.

"Dinner sounds great," she said softly.

He smiled broadly. "Phew," he said, mock wiping his brow. "I saw you bringing my wine and thought 'no way would a beautiful woman like that be available,' but I took a chance and I'm glad I did."

Sarah smiled, thinking about how she thought the same thing about him. "Yes, I'm definitely available," she said. "My schedule is wide open."

"Okay," he said. "Pick you up tomorrow at 6ish? Or do you like to eat later or earlier?"

"6 actually sounds perfect," Sarah said. Back in the day, she used to eat a 8 or even later, but, these days, she found late dinners did nothing but keep her awake, so she was grateful for the opportunity to have dinner early.

Oh, the things that had changed for her now that she was in her mid-50s.

She shyly gave him her address and he grinned broadly.

"Well, I need to settle my bill." Then he gave her his credit card, Sarah ran it, and he left a $200 tip. "I have to go," he said. "But I'll be seeing you tomorrow night."

"Tomorrow night," Sarah said dreamily.

Silas left and Sarah turned to Ava.

"Wow," was all she said.

Grab your copy...
vinci-books.com/beachfront-winery

About the Author

Ainsley Keaton lives with her hubby and two fur-babies in Southern California. When she's not binge-watching *Grace and Frankie, Succession* and *Downton Abbey*, she's reading historical and women's fiction and scouring the beach for sea glass and sand dollars.

www.ingramcontent.com/pod-product-compliance
Lightning Source LLC
La Vergne TN
LVHW030625241026
850939LV00032B/494
9781036703790